TRACK CHANGES

Also by Sayed Kashua

TRACK CHANGES

SAYED KASHUA

TRANSLATED FROM THE HEBREW
BY MITCH GINSBURG

Grove Press
New York

Published simultaneously in Canada
Printed in the United States of America

First Grove Atlantic hardcover edition: January 2020
First Grove Atlantic paperback edition: January 2021

This book is set in 12-point Cochin LT
by Alpha Design & Composition of Pittsfield, NH

Library of Congress Cataloging-in-Publication data is available for this title.

ISBN 978-0-8021-4845-2
eISBN 978-0-8021-4790-5

Grove Press
an imprint of Grove Atlantic
154 West 14th Street
New York, NY 10011

Distributed by Publishers Group West

groveatlantic.com

21 22 23 24   10 9 8 7 6 5 4 3 2 1

A

1

In the living room of a grad school dorm, I sat at a computer and stared at an old Sony tape player. It was the kind we used to call an executive recorder, and it was top-of-the-line when I bought it twenty years ago. I was so impressed with the name of the thing back then that I felt sure that my future—in management's top tier—was guaranteed. The recorder takes standard-size cassettes and has an external mic, three black buttons, and one red one for recording. I opened it gingerly with two fingers, making sure the tape was not tangled, and pulled out the ninety-minute Maxell cassette, B-side up. It was new, the plastic wrapping torn off just two months ago. I had known, already then, that I couldn't afford to take any chances, that it had to be a new cassette. Judging by the amount of magnetic tape spooled around the two white wheels, I had about sixty minutes of recording. I flipped the cassette, so that the A-side was up, peering at me through the clear deck window, and hit Rewind. The click of the black button, which popped up and stood even with the rest, informed me that I'd reached the beginning of the story.

For some reason this story starts at a bar in Chicago's O'Hare International Airport.

The bartender was pretty, and I was unable to guess where she was from. Not too dark, not too white. She must have been one of those people who can check multiple boxes on the ethnicity forms that Americans are asked to fill out when they sign their kids up for public school or open a bank account or visit a health clinic for the first time.

I sat on a high bar stool, tucking into my second beer. My carry-on suitcase was pressed against the side of the stool and every now and again I touched it offhandedly to ensure it was still in place. Noticing this, the bartender said that ever since airlines had started charging for stowed luggage anyone who can takes carry-on. "It saves twenty-five bucks," she said. "But it isn't really about the money, because a sandwich and a drink here cost about the same."

"Can I get a shot of Jameson?"

"A shot for eight or a double for twelve?" the bartender asked.

"Double, please," I said. "Neat." I had a total of five hundred dollars to cover the entire trip, and that had to include presents, however small, for the kids and maybe for Palestine, too.

"Here you go," the bartender said with a smile, and I smiled back. She was young and beautiful, or at least that's how I want to remember her. The age of servers and bartenders in America always surprised me, and I wasn't sure if it was a pleasant surprise or not. When we started taking the kids to local restaurants on the first Friday of every month, I started noticing that the servers and bartenders here can be old. In Jerusalem, they are always young, and the chance of finding a server over the age of thirty is possible only at what are called Oriental restaurants, which operate mostly

during the day. I didn't know what to make of the elderly
servers in America, who were sometimes in their sixties and
seventies. Sometimes I thought that it's good that there's no
age discrimination and hats off to the American public for
creating an equal opportunity job market. But other times
I felt a deep sorrow bubble up inside me when someone my
parents' age served me water in an ice-filled plastic cup—
with a wrapper-capped straw, of course—and said, "Here
you are, sir."

The cups of water in America are enormous, at least
in the usual chain restaurants, which are by and large what
we have in the small town where we live. My sons love TGI
Fridays and Buffalo Wild Wings. My daughter always says
she doesn't care where we go, that she'd rather skip the
whole scene and stay at home. And I say that I'd rather she
come along and join the rest of the family once a month,
that it's important, and she always relents. The servers in
these restaurants have a set routine. They deliver the tray
of cold water to the table and then hand out the menus and
ask if they can get you something to drink. The soft drinks
come in three sizes and the refills are free. Once they arrive
with the drinks, they expect you to be ready to order. First
courses and mains arrive together. Then they come back
once more and ask if everything's okay and if they can get
you anything else. Once you've said, "No, thanks, everything's fine," then they come back while you're still eating
and set the bill on the edge of the table, usually in a padded
folder with an inside pocket for the credit card. Around here
they don't wait for you to raise your finger and request the
bill. "Take your time, whenever you're ready," they always
say with a broad smile. Elderly servers, though, sadden

me, because it's hard work: you have to stay on your feet for hours on end, scurrying from kitchen to table, serving, seating, and cleaning. People of that age should be living a different life, free of the financial burdens that force people to work long shifts till they can no longer stand on their feet. I don't know why such things upset me, as though my life were so different from theirs. Maybe it's because I fear that their fate is what awaits me. After all, in order to buy the plane ticket, which cost over a thousand dollars, I had to use my wife's credit card, the Israeli one, and divide the payment into twelve equal installments, the most they'd let me do without interest.

The bartender's face showed no signs of distress. Sometimes I feel like I can read people's faces and know their backgrounds, their bank balances, and whether they were bullied or did the bullying during their school days. Sometimes I worry about the way in which others might read me.

I wanted a cigarette so badly, but in US airports there are no smoking corners whatsoever. The smoker is officially despised here, cigarettes the habit of beggars and criminals. Nonetheless, I asked the bartender, who said she was sorry, but no, there's no smoking zone here in O'Hare. But she'd heard that down South, in the Atlanta airport and others, they still had smoking rooms, somewhere after the security check. I looked at my cell and saw that I had an hour before boarding. I couldn't step out for a cigarette, though, because then I'd have to go back through security and although I knew I'd probably make it in time, I couldn't take the chance. I couldn't afford to take any undue risks, not today. The lines could be too long. I'll smoke in Paris, I figured. There had to be a smoking zone there and I had a two-hour layover in Charles de Gaulle before catching my connection to Tel Aviv.

I planned on nursing the whiskey. I couldn't afford another. Two beers and a double shot of whiskey ought to do the trick. I'll just drink slowly, I told myself, and save the last sip for the last minute. That way I'll board the plane with as much alcohol as possible in my bloodstream. And aside from cheap wine they don't offer beer or any other kind of alcohol on flights anymore, at least not in economy.

"So, where you off to?" the bartender asked.

There was no trace of an accent on her tongue, at least not a foreign one. I have an accent and always will. My ear is not attuned to the American vowel sounds and there are some words I don't even try to say like the locals, knowing in advance that I'll fail. And yet I can always recognize a foreign accent, in any language. People with a foreign accent carry a different expression on their faces, an expression that is hard to describe in words.

"Home," I said.

"Where's that at?"

"Jerusalem," I said, figuring that she must have heard of it and that it would spare me the rest of the explanations.

"Ohh, that's awesome, that's a place I've always wanted to visit. How long have you been away?"

"Almost two years. Actually, a bit more than two years."

"You live in Chicago?"

"Not remotely," I said, trying to be entertaining. "Urbana-Champaign."

"So, you're a Fighting Illini, then?" she asked.

"Go Illini," I said, masquerading as a foreign academic whose unique services had been sought by the university.

"You must miss it, though, huh?"

"Very much."

"You going home to let the family spoil you a bit?" she said with a sweet smile, asking a question suited to a younger man, not one fast approaching forty.

"Totally," I said, as the locals do.

"The food must be great over there, right?" she asked, and I nodded, "Best in the world."

"How long will you be abroad?"

"I don't know," I said.

I still didn't know.

2

The sky was starting to darken and the time on my phone showed ten in the morning as the plane touched down at Ben-Gurion International Airport. The American phone—its roaming data restricted to domestic use only—would not update to local time, 6:00 p.m., without a wireless connection. It had been more than twenty-four hours since I'd left my wife and our two boys for Tel Aviv. As for my daughter, well, I'd knocked softly on her door and called her name, but she had not come out of her room. Maybe she really had been asleep and hadn't heard.

A day before departure, I told the kids that I was going back to the old country for an important job. I told them that a rich customer had offered me a serious sum of money to write his autobiography. I told them I was going back simply to meet him and record his life story and that I'd do the rest of the work upon my return. My middle son asked me yet again what an autobiography was and when I explained it to him he still didn't understand why I write them for other people and why they don't write their own stories themselves.

I hugged the kids and promised to be back soon. My wife offered me a ride to the nearest bus stop and though I was happy for the offer, I declined, knowing that if she took me it would mean bringing the kids, too. And I believed that each and every car ride with the children, however brief, was a danger best avoided. I took the bus to Central Station and from there I took another to O'Hare.

As the plane taxied toward the terminal at Ben-Gurion I checked to see if there was a Wi-Fi connection. When we'd left the country, there had not been free internet at the airport, nor had we needed it. Back then we still had Israeli phones with a 3G package, which I'd asked the provider to cut at midnight on the night of our departure. That same night I searched online for my father's current cell phone number and wrote him a long text message to explain that we were going to the United States for work, that my wife and I had both been offered excellent opportunities, and we had decided to leave for a few years. We have three kids I also informed him: a daughter and two boys. And then we shut off our Israeli phones and boarded the plane.

Now I wanted to send my wife a short message. Just a quick: "How's it going?" containing no hint of longing or love. She'd understand that I'd landed and would respond with a soothing: "All good." Or if something had happened, she'd call.

One of the flight attendants reminded all passengers to stay buckled until the aircraft came to a full stop and the no-seatbelt sign had been turned off. The freedom to rise, as always, was announced with a ding, signaling the start of the race to the cabin doors. The goal was to exit as fast as possible, to push a single step closer to the doors. Seated in a window seat in one of the rear rows of the economy class, I had no choice but to shuffle aggressively forward like the rest of the passengers, as though a fire had seized the tail of the plane. I had to use my elbows to break into the current of traffic, otherwise I would have been the last person left on board. The race continued in the jet bridge that led to the terminal: the competition being to see who could get first to passport control, some moving in a fast gait, some at a full gallop. I tried not to join in but could not stop myself, for it is after all a war, and there is disdain here for the losers.

"Father's name?" asked the policewoman in the booth at the front of the Israeli passports line as she eyed my papers. I answered, and she handed over my passport with a slip permitting my entry to the country tucked into its pages. Once through passport control the passengers surged toward the duty-free counter, where the goods purchased upon departure were stocked in giant storage rooms, an arrangement that exists only in Israel's international airport.

Friends and family thronged the arrivals hall, eyeing the passengers as they came through the doors. Some clutched bunches of colorful balloons, and one young woman held a bouquet of flowers. I looked for the cigarettes I'd put in the front pocket of the suitcase and before lighting up I thought to myself, not for the first time, that if I'd managed to go without smoking for the duration of the flight it could well be the first step toward quitting. Maybe. I lit the cigarette and took a small drag, wary of the onset of dizziness, which strikes me whenever I first smoke after an hours-long break. I hoped that I didn't stink of alcohol and that the smoke would help cover the tracks of the drinking I'd done during my layover at de Gaulle, where I'd also smoked as much as I could in the glass cage that I shared with the other similarly condemned passengers, whose Arabic came in an array of dialects.

January—and darkness comes early.

The weather, though, was nice, even quite warm when compared to the Midwest. I didn't need the jacket I'd brought. A sweater would have sufficed.

Walking toward the taxi stand, I cupped my palm over my mouth and sniffed but was unable to say definitively what my breath smelled like. The first taxi driver in line waited outside his car and cast me a hurrying look. He smiled a forced smile in my direction and popped the trunk. "No need," I told him. "It's only a small bag."

"As you like," he said in a Russian accent.

I sat on the right side of the back seat and set my bag down to my left.

I wondered if the driver was scared and promptly found myself immersed in all of the old fears. Nothing had changed. I did not want to trigger feelings of anger, suspicion, or discomfort in a Jewish driver with a Russian accent who was in the process of discovering that he was transporting an Arab. It's possible the matter would cause not so much as a flutter of excitement and that he regularly drives Arabs to villages within the Green Line and that he is one of the many Israelis who makes the pilgrimage to Tira on Shabbat for the weekend market, which I learned about only a few years ago from an Israeli TV program. A market that draws thousands of Israelis every Saturday to the city, which I will always call a village, searching for a variety of food and

merchandise and principally looking to spend their day of
rest in the fanciful atmosphere of financial prudence, cling-
ing with blind faith to the notion that all things Arab are
by definition cheap. And what reason would the taxi driver
have for fearing to enter an Arab town in Israel proper?
True, he has a Russian accent, but the accent seemed like a
function of age and not a reflection on the number of years
he'd been in the country. If there's a formula that can take
the two variables, age upon immigration and accent, I'd use
it in order to estimate that he had made aliya twenty years
ago. He certainly works with Arab drivers, knows to dif-
ferentiate between different sorts of Palestinians, probably
has already learned to say a few words in Arabic, and yet I
was incapable of saying to him that I wanted to go to Tira,
the site of my birth, home to my parents and siblings, whom
I have not seen in years. I was not able to say to him that
I wanted to go home and take a shower, remove the yoke
of foreignness, change clothes, and rest from the twenty-
four hours of travel before embarking on the assignment
for which I had come. Instead I asked him to take me to
Kfar Saba, speaking the name of the city in a way that any
native Israeli would recognize and categorize but not this
driver, who as a new immigrant lacked those skills, even if
his newness was two decades old.

"We'll take Route Six?" the driver seemed to both state
and ask. "It's fastest, because Route Four's backed up. By
the way, are you a smoker? I saw you smoking before."

"Yes."

"You can smoke in the cab, no problem. Just open the
window."

"Thank you."

"I quit ten years ago. I used to smoke two packs a day. I kicked it one day and since then, nothing, ten years not a single cigarette. But you know what? I still like the smell, and I still miss the cigarettes."

I pressed the button and lowered the window halfway before even starting to smoke. Cold air brushed past my face and I tried to gauge, by its touch, the extent of my longing. I tried to inhale deeply, to smell the country, because I'd read in several books that the sense of smell is the sense of longing. I'd always read about people who recalled the scent of the earth, the oranges, the air, and the sea. I tried, but my nose did not detect any special scent, did not tap into any wellspring of memory, perhaps because the smell of the highway from the airport to Route 6 was not the smell of my childhood or my homeland as I knew it.

Was this a betrayal? I blamed my own inadequacies for my nose not picking up the scent of longing that I'd read about in the poems. And then I rejected the accusation. No, I didn't have to pick up certain scents in order to prove that I had longed; I didn't have to prove anything to anyone. For many years I had yearned for home and thought of returning every day, shirking the misery of foreignness and the sadness of detachment.

When I reach Tira, the familiar smell of home will surely assault my senses, scents of childhood and nettles after the rain. When I walk into my parents' house, I'll definitely burst into tears when my father's smell—which will forever be a blend of Old Spice and cigarettes—engulfs me.

3

"What's your earliest memory?"

That was the question I asked interviewees as soon as I hit the red Record button on the recorder.

What's my earliest memory? Sometimes I ask myself, too.

I remember my mother waking me up in the middle of the night, frightened and stressed, hoisting me onto her shoulders. And I remember insisting on taking my new box of crayons with me, stretching my hand out toward the place under my pillow where I'd hidden them, but I couldn't reach. We've got to hurry. The buses are heading out soon, and we must drive my grandmother to the center of the village, to the square outside the old Bank Hapoalim, where we'll wave goodbye to her and the others as they set out on the haj, the first group to be granted exit visas to Mecca.

Or maybe it's a memory of my back pressed against the low wall that surrounded the first kindergarten in Tira, in a part of the neighborhood far from my home, which my parents decided to send me to because of their jobs. I'm leaning against the wall and staring at some kids playing with metal toy cars with small seats and squeaky steering wheels that can spin endlessly in either direction. Close to me are seesaws in the shape of a horse and a plane, and a sandbox. I look at the other kids and cry, waiting for the moment when my parents will come and get me and failing to understand why the other kids are not, like me, standing with their backs to the wall and wailing until their parents arrive. Slowly I discover that the kindergarten teacher is standing beside me, looking over the wall. It takes me some time to realize that she is talking about me when she says, "He's always like this. He doesn't play or listen to stories or speak to any of the other kids." And I look back and see that she is talking to my father, who is standing right behind me on the other side of the white brick wall. I turn to look at him and he smiles at me, tousles my hair, and waves the gray handkerchief that we are all required to carry. "You forgot this," he says and smiles at me.

I have no doubt that both of these events took place. I don't know which came first but I regurgitate them often. I don't have a lot of childhood memories other than those two, and I haven't been able to bring up new ones, aside from those that have been carved into the walls of my mind, in a spot where the beam of my memory repeatedly falls. Those things happened; I will not even entertain the notion that they did not, even though it is unclear to me how it is that I see myself in both of those distant memories. How is it that I see the kid crying rather than being there myself, my back against the wall; how is it that I watch the kid with the leaping heart see his father, a kid that is no longer me?

Soon, when we get close to Tira, I'll smell the trees, the clouds, the strawberries, and the figs that I used to pick with my father, even though it is not fig season and the place where the trees once stood is now home to a row of exhaust pipe garages.

4

"Is here, okay?" the cabby asked. "Or do you want me to go all the way to the gate?"

"Here's great," I said when I saw that we had reached the entrance to Meir Hospital in Kfar Saba.

The taxi pulled to a stop, facing north, in the direction of Tira. Five more minutes and I could've been at home. I looked to the right to make sure that the share taxis connecting Kfar Saba and Tira were still parked in the same spot as they had been fourteen years ago when I last boarded one of the passenger vans. And there they were, only now with an official taxi sign, making the once-unlicensed stop official.

"One hundred and seventy shekels," the Russian driver said, reminding me that I didn't have any Israeli currency.

"I'm so sorry," I said, flipping through my wallet and waiting for a miracle that would transform my American bills into Israeli shekels. "Is fifty dollars okay?"

"Even better," he said, and I handed him the bill without waiting for change, even though I knew that in Israel drivers are not tipped.

As I crossed the street in its direction, Meir Hospital looked bigger than I remembered: a few new buildings had been added, and there was now a little security hut and a metal turnstile at the entrance.

There was no chance of me getting through the turnstile with my trolley suitcase.

"Wait for the security guard," a young man with an Arab accent behind me said, and I tried to check and see if he was from Tira or if he noticed that I was from Tira, though he had addressed me in Hebrew. People from Tira recognize one another. "I'll tell the guard," he said as he pushed through the turnstile.

"Where to?" the guard asked before clicking open the door to the security hut.

"I'm visiting my father."

"Which ward?"

"Cardiac."

"Cardiac Institute's in the tower."

"Is that in the new building?"

The guard had no idea what I was talking about; as far as he was concerned the tower had always been there, built before he was even born. I pointed toward the building, which must have been erected more than three decades ago, and the security guard nodded.

Meir Hospital. In Arabic we tweaked the name, never using the word "mustashfa" — hospital — and Arabizing the other word with a long *a* sound: Maaer. "He got a referral to Maaer," we'd say, because without a referral from the local health clinic, you couldn't just show up at the hospital, aside from in true emergencies. And a referral to Maaer, back when we were little, was something to be proud of, a sign that you really had hurt yourself. I was once referred to Maaer after I'd injured my foot. It had turned blue and swollen and the local doctor, saying I needed an X-ray, had printed out a referral to the hospital. The X-ray, though, revealed no sign of a fracture and I was deeply sorry that there were no broken bones and that I had apparently wasted my father's time.

When I got older I would sometimes accompany him on visits to see hospitalized relatives. Back in the day those visits were obligatory, and relatives would spend days packed into the corners of hospital waiting rooms. The women would bring food and the men would supply fresh coffee. Once, when I was in high school, I was left at the bedside of my maternal uncle, who had been in a bad car accident with his son and was in critical condition. After an all-night operation, my uncle's condition improved and the next morning he opened his eyes and started to talk. When he asked about his son, everyone told him, "Alhamdulillah, he's okay." When he asked to see his son, those at his bedside told him that he was being treated nearby, in Petach Tikva, and that he would be fine and that what was most important now was that he focus on his own recuperation. My uncle didn't know that his son had been killed in the crash. On the day of the funeral, all of the men from the village had to participate in the ceremony but they didn't want to leave my uncle alone, so they asked me, as an already-mature and rather smart kid, a "good kid," to stay by his bedside until the funeral was over and the mourning tent had been built. They said that they trusted me and that my uncle must not know that he had lost his son because his condition was still unstable, and that only once he'd recuperated from the surgery would one of the adults come and tell him that his firstborn child had died.

"Why hasn't your aunt come to visit?" he asked me as soon as it was just the two of us alone in the hospital room.

"I don't know, Uncle," I told him. "She's probably with Omar in Petach Tikva."

"If your aunt hasn't come to see me and is with him constantly then he must be in really bad condition."

"No, Uncle," I said. "No, she was here when you were being operated on. She left just before you came to."

"Have you seen him?" he asked, and I, who only that morning had seen Omar's body, answered that I had and that he was "fine, totally fine. He even asked about you, and then we played that game that he likes with the chutes and the ladders. He beat me four to one."

"Yes, he likes that game," my uncle said and smiled. "You know, you're the only one I really believe. Now I can relax. I thought the adults were lying to me. Adults always lie."

"Never, Uncle," I said. "I never ever lie." And I swore to God.

I tugged the trolley bag along gently, making sure the wheels didn't rattle too much as I crossed the entryway to the new wing of the hospital.

It was seven in the evening here, eleven in the morning in Illinois. Sunday morning—my children would all be at home. I hoped they didn't go out, that my wife wouldn't put the kids at risk. "How the hell is going to the library putting the children at risk?" I heard her argue with me. Just please don't let it snow today, I thought, for my wife has no qualms about driving the kids around even when it's snowing. She doesn't know about black ice, and she isn't willing to hear a word about how quickly people die because of it. "Everyone's driving," I can hear her say as I walk toward the block of elevators at the entry level, asserting vehemently that were it up to me, the entire state would be shut down at the first sign of snow.

Seven in the evening is when the stores on the ground floor close. A young saleswoman from the gift store was bringing in a metal wagon on which there were balloons that read "Mazel Tov" and "Get Well Soon." The grate in front of the bookstore was being shut, too, and only the café across the way, a franchise of a larger chain, was still open. It dawned on me that I should have brought my father a present. After all I hadn't seen him in fourteen years.

"The Cardiology Institute?" a tired woman in her fifties in a pair of green scrubs asked as she came out of the elevator. She looked like a nurse, but I wasn't sure I was able to categorize hospital employees by their garb. When I was little I thought that in a hospital only doctors wore scrubs, but little by little I realized that even the floor cleaners, who sometimes greeted us in Arabic, or the guy with the limp pushing the empty wagons, wore some sort of scrubs.

"Cardiology's on the fourth floor."

5

My father is small. My father is pale. My father's eyes are sunken deep in their sockets. I look at him and try to follow his inhalations, tracing the rise and fall of his chest as the respirator pumps air in and out, recognizing the exact moment when his lungs fill up and empty, watching for movement, however slight, beneath the thin, Star of David–patterned sheet that covers him. That's what I did with each of my kids when they were babies, what I still do with my youngest son before I leave his bedside every night, even though he's nearly five. When I can't see visible signs of respiration, I bring my ear to his mouth and listen, eyes shut. And if I don't hear anything, I draw even closer, to feel his warm breath against my right cheek.

I'd like to feel my father's breath on my cheek, but the oxygen mask prevents me from doing so.

I have been so scared of this moment, so preoccupied with it. Ever since I can remember starting to remember, my father's death is what I've feared most. In all of the dark scenarios I conjured, it was always his heart that gave out, even before I understood the danger of the cigarettes he smoked.

"Heart attack," I'd hear people say in my youth, when speaking of a sudden death. "Heart attack," back then meant

certain death. When I was little I didn't even know it was
possible to live after one. "Sakta qalbiya," they would say,
and to me the phrase sounded like the falling of the heart:
"Sakta qalbiya," and how can you go on living after the
heart has fallen out.

"What happened to me?" my father asked in a soft voice
once he'd pulled down his oxygen mask. "You had a heart
attack, Dad," I answered softly, and I could see in his eyes
he started to remember.

"Is that you? When did you get here?" He tried to
smile.

"I came in the evening. You were asleep."

"What time is it?"

"Two."

"In the morning?"

"Yes."

"How're your wife and your kids?"

"They send regards."

"They're in Tira?"

"No. I came alone."

"Have you been to the house?"

"Not yet."

"Can you get me some water?" he said with a dry throat
as he tried to wet his lips with his tongue. There was a bottle
of water on his bedside table. I brought the bottle to his lips.
He was able to raise his head, and he opened his mouth with
difficulty. I could see no way of offering him a drink without
pouring some into his mouth.

"What are you doing?" a nurse scolded me in a Russian accent as she walked into the room. "Are you trying
to kill him?"

She flung open a drawer and pulled out a black straw. "Here, slowly, put this in his mouth and he can drink. Slowly."

I did as she instructed and Dad gently pursed his lips and sucked up some water.

"No," I told the nurse in a whisper, trying to control my voice so that the rage pulsing in my temples would not be exposed.

"No, what?" the nurse asked.

"No, ma'am, I am not trying to kill my father."

"What?" she snapped impatiently. She had no idea what I was talking about. "When he's done drinking put the oxygen mask back in place, okay?"

~~"You've already killed me anyway," I imagined his whisper.~~

My father fell back asleep. Was it the same sleep that he once treasured? The same sleep that he would announce the commencement of on Saturday afternoons and that we would have to respect, keeping quiet, refraining from running around the house, slamming doors, bouncing balls out in the yard. The sleep the violation of which, we knew, might well bring punishment? Is the sleep of one who's dazed by medicine akin to the sleep of one who sleeps in his bed? Is the sleep of one who prepares ceremoniously for it, showering, brushing teeth, urinating, and putting on pajamas, or perhaps remaining in his underwear, akin to an imposed sleep? Are the dreams of those in the hospital identical to the dreams of those in their beds?

"What do you think about when you get into bed?" was one of the standard questions that I asked my clients. Generally, people said they thought about the things they were supposed to find truly important: their kids, their grandkids, their wives, their countries. That was why I asked them. I never expected them to say anything except what they would like to be remembered for after their deaths.

The written memory must be made beautiful, and if I felt that the material I was given during an interview might tarnish the image of the protagonist of the memoir in the eyes of his or her readers, I edited their dreams, erased and added sentences, and even, as necessary, invented new dreams and new thoughts to accompany them in bed. I inserted into their life stories memories and dreams that they had never dreamt or recalled and, generally, when I sent them a draft for approval and correction, they liked the reflections they saw and were convinced the words were faithful renditions of the truth as they had experienced it, accurate depictions of the way they drifted into sleep.

One of the first people to hire me to write his life story told me that ever since he'd moved into an old-age home his technique for summoning sleep was to conjure every woman he had ever desired. Those memories, he said, are his most beautiful ones and they bring him a sense of joy even though they are often memories of unrequited lust. Every night he starts at the beginning, from first crushes in grade school, and moves forward chronologically until he loses the thread or falls asleep, whatever comes first. I transcribed the memory word for word from the recording, and then I highlighted and erased it. Although I did not put it in his memoir, which was full of stories of valor from the many battles in which he had fought, it's the only story of his that my memory has saved.

6

What do I think about before I fall asleep?

Back in the day, when I'd have trouble getting to sleep, I'd imagine myself as a soldier, even though I've never been in an army and have never held a gun that isn't a toy. I was clad in army green but didn't know in whose ranks I was fighting. During those presleep, imaginary war games I manned a defensive position, usually guarding the house. The war always took place in the vicinity of the house, not far from the bed in which I slept. Actually, in my mind, I lay in a trench, covered in mud, trying to stop the advance of a faceless and nameless enemy, sticking small grenades in the treads of hulking tanks, scurrying from hideout to hideout in the neighborhood that I knew so well, employing to my advantage my perfect knowledge of the battlefield. Bullets whistled past my ears but never hit me, and every shot I fired found its mark.

When I was a kid, I defended my home in Tira; when I became a father, I defended our home in Jerusalem; but when I moved to Illinois, I wasn't able to defend a thing. I didn't know where to hide, where the forces were positioned, where the enemy assault would come from.

My attempts at lulling myself to sleep while imagining myself as a soldier defending the family home no longer worked. Back in the day I would emerge victorious from every battle or at least fall asleep while still maintaining the perimeter, the enemy unable to strike the home I was in. But ever since the move to Illinois I surrender before the battle has even begun, a surrender to the brigades of insomnia.

My mother and my older brother and his wife, whom I was meeting for the first time, shared a bench outside my father's hospital room. My mother's eyes were swollen from crying, and her sobbing intensified when she saw me. "Why didn't you tell me you were coming?" she cried and seemed not to know if she was allowed to hug me.

~~"What are you doing here?" my older brother asked. "Why'd you come?"~~

~~"Stop it," my mother ordered. "Not now, not in the hospital. He's your brother. Enough."~~

~~"You smelled death and came to take some of the remains?" my brother said. And Mom cried and begged in the name of Allah that this was not the time, that we are brothers.~~

~~"Enough," my brother's wife said, too, taking his hand. "You want to make a scene in the hospital?"~~

~~"Go home," my mother urged him and turned to his wife. "Please, take your husband home."~~

~~"Let's go," his wife said, tugging his hand. "Let's go home."~~

When I first arrived at the hospital, my mother accompanied me to the room in the intensive care section of the cardiology ward, where my father's shrunken body lay, hooked up to masks and wires, as a metallic rectangular machine filled and emptied his lungs at a predetermined rate. I didn't know if I was allowed to approach him, touch him, hug him, or hold his hand as I'd seen in the movies. In the end I touched him gently, but he didn't respond.

Mom filled me in on the medical details, which I did not fully understand. I managed to grasp that they'd taken him to the hospital due to weakness, vomiting, and intense back pain. And that at first they didn't know what was wrong and simply wanted to monitor him and run a few tests, but during those first days his condition worsened and on the morning of my arrival he was stricken with sharp pains in his chest. An EKG showed he was having an acute heart attack, and he was taken to the operating room for a heart catheterization in two arteries or maybe it was veins. I'm not sure. ~~My mother also said that in the interim the tests from before the heart attack started to come back, and they showed that my father has an advanced stage of lung cancer, which has already spread to the bones and the liver.~~

"How's your wife? And the kids? I understand you already have two?"

"Three. A girl and two boys. They're okay, they send regards."

"How'd you find us?"

"I asked at information," I told her, even though I knew she meant: Who told you? How did you know? Who are you even in touch with?

I didn't tell her that my father, two days earlier, had sent me a short message over Skype, right after I'd accepted his friendship request. He only wrote, "I'm in the hospital," but I knew right away it was his heart.

My mother encouraged me to go home, take a shower, eat, rest up after the long journey, but I insisted on staying by my father's bed. After all, that was the reason I'd come, the reason I'd asked Palestine for permission to buy a plane ticket, explaining to her that the situation was grave and even lying and saying that I'd spoken to my father's attending physician in the hospital, who said that if he were me he would come back immediately. She consented. She would have done so without the lie, too, allowing me to go over our budget and break our unwritten agreements, signed, over the years, in long silences.

I've come the whole way just to be by his side, I practically begged my mother, even though I knew she wasn't sure if she ought to leave me with my father.

"My body's still ticking on an American clock," I told her, because I wanted her to go already. "Tomorrow, tomorrow morning I'll come home," I promised her, hoping I would manage to keep my promise.

7

My father's condition, the doctors say, is critical but stable.
From Mom's explanation I was able to grasp that after the catheterization Dad's lungs filled with fluid and he wasn't able to breathe. They hooked him up to a respirator and drained the liquid from his lungs. After a few hours, during which they thought they might lose him, the doctors were able to take him off the respirator and leave him hooked up only to the oxygen mask. Mom said it was important to keep an eye on the oximeter, and she showed me how to read the screen. "If it goes under eighty," she said, "call the nurse immediately." Another thing I had to keep an eye on was the nearly empty urine drainage bag, which dangled over the side of the bed. "When he starts expelling," my mother said, claiming to have discussed this in detail with one of the cardiologists from Tira who works at Meir Hospital, "we'll know that he's getting better. An excellent cardiologist, that Ahmad, do you know him? He was in your grade. Maybe one grade behind you. He helped us a lot today. If he swings by, be on your best behavior and be grateful, although I doubt he'll come because senior physicians don't work night shifts."

I watched the saturation levels on the oximeter, though I did not understand their significance. Sometimes they went up to ninety-two and sometimes they went down to eighty-five. The monitor, which presented my father's condition in shimmering graphs and flickering numbers and lights, started to beep, and a nurse entered the room, silenced the beeping with the pressing of a button, and then turned down the volume of the machine to practically zero. Had she not silenced it, it would probably have continued beeping, because a red light flashed incessantly. I did not inquire of the nurse what the beeps and silences meant; I figured they knew their trade and I didn't want to interfere.

I returned to the couch, which was positioned beneath the large window that spanned the length of the room and looked out on a high-rise construction site. It was now six in the evening in Illinois. My wife had responded to me earlier to say that everything was okay and that I should "pass on her warmest get-well wishes." My youngest son was probably in the bath at this stage of the evening, and I figured I'd send him a message later, once he'd put on his superhero pajamas and was getting ready for bed. Usually I'm there with him till he falls asleep. Maybe I'll even talk to him a little bit later, I thought. My daughter will be up later than the boys, but there's not much chance she'll want to talk to me. The weather app showed it to be ten degrees in Illinois and fifty in Kfar Saba. With a single tap I changed it from Fahrenheit to Celsius, which seemed more appropriate here. No snow predicted for tomorrow in Illinois and a light rain possible in Kfar Saba.

The nurse popped into the room once an hour, and each time she stepped in I stood up. She looked at my father, at the instruments and monitors, noted the urine volume in the bag, and jotted down some figures on the clipboard attached to the foot of the hospital bed.

"You can get yourself something to drink, if you want," the nurse said, surprising me at close to five in the morning by addressing me directly. "There's a little kitchenette there with coffee and tea, some bread, and cottage cheese and chocolate spread in the fridge."

"Thanks so much," I said apologetically, in light of the earlier incident, after I'd tried to give my father a drink straight from the bottle.

"Did you just get in?" she asked, tilting her head in the direction of the trolley suitcase in the corner of the ICU room.

"In the evening," I said, and she nodded once and left the room.

It's been two years since I've had black coffee from one of those red-and-black bags labeled "Turkish Coffee." That was the coffee I used to have every morning in Jerusalem: two spoonsful, half a cup of hot water, a splash of milk, no sugar. I used to drink it in the newsroom, too, a cup almost hourly.

I didn't find any Styrofoam cups in the kitchenette and didn't want to bother the nurse, so I took two plastic cups from the water cooler and doubled them up so that they wouldn't collapse from the heat. In the United States they don't have this sort of cup, which is too thin, too see-through, too small, and so feeble they need to be held gingerly around the rim lest they fold in your hand. I walked slowly, cautious with the sloshing liquid, to the room where my father lay, in order to make sure that he had not woken up before I abandoned him for a cigarette.

✼   ✼   ✼

On the ground floor, the square in front of the stores was empty. A young Arab man, not dressed in hospital scrubs, slowly pushed a large floor buffer, and over the hum of the machinery I could hear him singing along to a tune wafting out of his phone, which he had laid flat over the top of the machine. I didn't recognize the song—it was new, apparently—and the hum of the machine prevented me from identifying the singer.

The notion that I hadn't heard a single Arabic song since I left bothered me, as though I'd forgotten that I like Arabic music, if not the new stuff then at least the classics I used to hear in my parents' house and that I loved in my childhood, detested in my adolescence, and am once again moved by in middle age. Surely there are a slew of singers that the young generation loves and that I haven't even heard of, stars I don't even know well enough to hate. And my kids? Do they even know a single Arab singer? Can they even recognize Umm Kulthum or Abdel Halim? When I get back I'll be sure to play Arabic music for them. I'll start with Fairuz—my father loved her voice so much—the children's songs or maybe that song about Jerusalem. The kids must know that one, they must know it.

I evaded the floor cleaner and hoped he hadn't seen me. You can't step on the floor while it's being cleaned. You have to wait until the water has fully dried and then wipe your shoes rigorously on the mat or the rag before stepping inside the house. Otherwise Mom is angry. The premorning air was cool, and I regretted not taking my jacket. Sometimes

it seems to me that it is always cold at this time of day, ir-
respective of season and geography.

I sat down on a wooden bench along the divide between
the old and new wings of the hospital and slowly brought
the plastic cup to my mouth, tilting the coffee gently toward the brim so that the hot liquid just grazed my lips
as I tested the temperature. Once I was sure the liquid
would not scald my tongue, I blew into the cup, puckered
my lips, and sucked up some of the hot coffee. The deeply
familiar taste made me momentarily dizzy and I was not
able to fully interpret the sensation: a swirl of memories,
either pleasant or cruel. I shivered and placed the cup of
coffee on the asphalt floor and threaded my right hand up
beneath the sleeve of my sweater and felt the hairs bristling
on my left arm. I lit a cigarette, took a long drag and held
the smoke in my lungs until I released it with an equally long
exhalation. The flashing lights of a muted ambulance siren
cut through the morning air, the parking barricade rose to
a vertical position, and the ambulance accelerated to the
front of the old building. The ER was still in the same spot.
There was no sense of unusual urgency in the actions of the
paramedics, who set the gurney down and rolled it inside. I
couldn't see the face of the prone person, but I noticed that
aside from the paramedics in uniform a young woman in a
sweat suit stepped out of the ambulance, her back hunched
and her arms locked across her chest. Behind me, once the
stir of commotion was still, I heard whispering and turned
my head. A young man stood at the foot of a dusky stairwell
and looked as though he were hiding, popping his head out
every now and again to make sure he was safe and whispering
some unclear words in Arabic into his phone, a wide smile

spread across his face. I managed to note that he was wearing a brown shirt similar to the one worn by the floor cleaner and decided they worked for the same employment agency. I imagined the young cleaner whispering on the phone to his beloved, who had woken up at dawn or perhaps had not gone to sleep at all, and she whispering back to him from bed so that no one would hear, or maybe she was actually silent. After all, what were the chances that she would have a room of her own and not one shared by sisters and other family members. I imagined her trying to keep silent, smiling, perhaps under the covers, listening to the young man in the brown shirt, her heart pounding with fright and hope. How jealous I was of the two contracted workers, who would undoubtedly finish their shifts and return home, to the homes in which they were born, never running the risk of disorientation while returning. I was jealous of the man who had no doubt about where he would build his home, where he would raise his children, in which soil he will be interred when he dies.

The envy quickly morphed into pain for what I had done to Palestine, a pain that I tried to dull with a big sip of coffee and a harsh drag off the cigarette. Oh, Tira, Tira, I will have to return. I must right that which I once wronged. I'll get on my knees in the center of the village and will beg forgiveness from every passerby, from those who know the story and from those who've never heard my name.

"Just wanted to say good night," I wrote to my wife in an SMS, without expecting a response.

Soon my mother will return to the hospital and relieve me, and I'll go back to the house to sleep in the same childhood

bed beneath the same window where I would put the pillow, so that I could look out until I could no longer keep
my eyes open, ready for the worst, ears attuned to every
sound, every movement.

I was always the last of my three brothers, my roommates, to close my eyes. I didn't know how they could just let
themselves fall asleep like that. Did they not hear the same
stories that I heard from the neighbors? The one about the
demon who appears at times as a girl or as a cat? How could
they possibly fall asleep, particularly during those warm
summer nights, when there was no choice but to leave the
window open? People forget that there were no air condi-
tioners back then, certainly not in Tira. Summer nights were
hot, but the heat was bearable as long as the windows were
open in a way that allowed a cross breeze. Americans don't
open the windows at all, not in the steamy summer and not
in the freezing winter. Not in the autumn and not in the
spring. And I, like them, have learned to seal myself in and
keep the air-conditioning turned to its appropriate setting.

Soon I'll be home, and the windows will surely be shut
on account of winter. And the winter nights in Tira are especially cold in my recollection. First contact with the mattress
was always painful and you had to inhale sharply and ball
up beneath the covers until the bed was warmed. Soon I'll
be there and will once again be able to feel the caress of the
mattress and the wool blanket. Then I'll shut my eyes and
again become the most devoted soldier I've ever been, a
soldier who knows the best hiding places, the ones that no
foreign invader could ever find.

B

1

Two months have passed since that trip. It's now mid-March and the temperature is still close to zero degrees, Fahrenheit.

I plug the earphones into the jack on the recorder, even though I'm alone and no one can hear. I press Play and the small plastic wheel starts to turn. A whispery quiet—and then my voice.

"Your first memory?"

"I didn't bring you here from America to talk about my first memory."

My father's voice reverberated in my ears and a tremor radiated up from my toes, a new sensation, a wave that surged up through my body and broke in my throat and eyes. I stopped the cassette and cried for the first time. A different sort of crying, unrecognizable to me—a wailing that I tried to stifle with a pillow. The kids, I had to check in on the kids. I'll call Palestine, I figured, even though it's already after midnight. She was definitely asleep, but I'd have to wake her. It wasn't the worst crime; she'd have to understand. I'll just ask her to check on the kids, see that they're breathing. Or maybe I won't wake her. I'll just go over there. I'll take a bus. I'll ride over and see my children, make sure they're okay, that they're alive. No one will notice. But there are no buses at this hour. So I would have to walk, a brisk fifteen-minute stroll, at most half an hour.

I'll put on my thermal underwear and long coat, a scarf
and wool hat, and march over to the house to see my kids.
First, though, I have to get control of this sobbing, catch my
breath, smooth out the jagged inhalations, calm the storm
that caught me unprepared, shattering the windows that I
forgot to board up. She'll definitely understand, my wife. I
simply have to call her.

I called the first of two numbers on my Favorites list
and hung up immediately. She's probably asleep and tomorrow she has a long day, as usual. I texted the second number
on my list. "You up?" I asked my daughter in Hebrew, hoping she wouldn't lose the only language in which she once
knew how to read. She answered right away. "Yeah, what's
going on?" she wrote, in English.

I called her cell and she answered. "Are you okay?" I
asked in Arabic, a language she comprehends only in the
Palestinian field-workers' dialect that we spoke at home.

"Yes," she answered in Hebrew and then in English:
"I'm fine."

"Are your brothers okay? Your mother?"

"Did something happen?"

"No, nothing. Just checking," I told her, even though I
wanted to say that she has a grandfather, that I have a father
and mother and a village and family. "Sorry, I'm just writing
a bit and suddenly, you know, just do me a favor, please, and
go into your brothers' room and check that they're okay.
Sometimes when I'm writing I imagine all sorts of nightmare
scenarios."

"They're fine. I'm not going into anyone's room."

"Please, otherwise I'll have to come over," I begged. I
asked that she stay on the line as she goes into their room.

"They're asleep," she whispered.

"Can you do me a favor and just put the phone next to your little brother's mouth, as if he's speaking to me?"

I held my breath, perking my ears to pick up the child's respirations but heard nothing.

"Okay," my daughter said. "He's starting to wake up, so I think we're done here."

"He's moving?"

"Yes!" she yelled in a whisper. "I have to get back to my room Bye." She hung up.

They're okay. The little one is the one who worries me. It's always the littlest that generates the most amount of anxiety, and my daughter said that he had moved, that he practically woke up, so he's okay.

I stepped out onto the kitchen balcony to smoke, this time without gloves, in the hopes that the cold would shock me back to my surroundings and still the rhythm of my breathing.

I ground the cigarette out in the bucket of frozen water and returned to the desk, where I opened a new file: "Dad Transcript."

2

Back when we lived in Jerusalem, I always woke up before my wife and kids. I liked that hour of early morning quiet. In Illinois the situation is different. I want to sleep late, to avoid waking up, as has long been my habit.

The winter mornings here are icy and dark. I try to stay still in bed, hoping for the sun to come up. I try to think about the book I have to write, about the first-person protagonist that is the me character. But swiftly I'm seized by harsh thoughts that force me out of bed to start my morning routine, rituals meant to banish the demons.

Coffee is my first task. It took me several long months to get used to the idea and the taste of American coffee, coffee that until we came here I had seen only on TV and in movies. A white filter, four heaped tablespoons, four cups of water in the designated slot, a transparent glass pot, set in its ring—and then the flipping of a switch to start the process. Only then do I go urinate. Even if my bladder is pressing I will always start the coffee machine before going to the bathroom. Ten minutes will pass before it's ready, and I have to make the most of my time.

I've now developed a fondness for American coffee. I take the first two cups with milk, with the firm belief that the lactose gets the intestinal track moving. After going to the bathroom, I put on my two-ply winter coat—the inner layer providing insulation and the outer layer serving as a sort of wind and rain guard. We bought these coats together, for the whole family, over two years ago, once we understood that without proper winter coats a person could freeze to death here in ten minutes. In Israel there's no need for special coats, not even in Jerusalem, which is considered especially cold.

Before zipping up the coat I pull on some thick thermal socks and then step into waterproof boots, another local purchase, and wrap a wool scarf around my neck and pull a hat down over my ears. I put a glove on my left hand but leave my right one bare, so that I can pour coffee into a travel mug, and then add only a touch of milk so that the coffee doesn't cool down too much. Smoking is prohibited inside — actually it's prohibited everywhere on campus — including the graduate student dorms and the faculty housing for visiting academics.

During our first few weeks in town, I'd walk down one of the side streets with my coffee and cigarette in hand, but as the weather got colder I started smoking on the path that leads from the kitchen to the stairs. I smoke fast in the winter, three minutes per cigarette at most. Otherwise my hand goes numb. Afterward I grind the cigarettes into a bucket of frozen water, enjoying the hissing sound that the burning cigarettes make upon impact with the ice.

3

Whenever people ask me: "What are you doing in Illinois?" I always say that I'm writing a book, even though ever since we've arrived I've not written a single word.

To be honest, I've only been asked this a few times, mostly at social events held by the department where my wife is teaching, events that family and spouses are specifically invited to and that she, having told her colleagues that she's married, was compelled to request I accompany her to, knowing full well that I would not pass on an opportunity to feel like we were in a relationship.

"So, you're a writer?"

I lie because I have nothing better to say.

Albeit I've written thirty books but only as a hired hand. Aside from one short story, less than a page long and featured in the Hebrew University students' journal some fifteen years ago, I've not published a single piece of writing under my own name, and even then the editor misspelled my first name, adding a guttural vowel where there was none.

Sometimes I think about my book, the one I promised I would never write, and I imagine the protagonist in a furnished one-room apartment in the University of Illinois dorms.

Around here they only count bedrooms when specifying the number of rooms in an apartment. He lives alone, this protagonist, in the married-student dorms. He has a small bedroom, in the middle of which sits a queen-size bed on an appropriately sized box mattress, with no headboard. He has a closet, which is nothing more than an accordion-like door that opens to a narrow, carpeted, shelf-less space that houses a single hanging bar, fixed at the protagonist's eye level, five foot seven.

In his apartment there's also a living room and a three-seater couch, an old TV with cable access, and a desk made out of sturdy wood. In that same open space there is also a small kitchen and a refrigerator, a stove and an electric stovetop, a microwave and a coffee machine. It was all there when I moved in; I bought no new furniture aside from some plastic shelves that I got at one of the giant hardware stores, a translucent set of storage drawers that are bought individually and can be assembled any which way, like Lego. I placed them one on top of another and shoved them into my bedroom closet. The bottom one is for socks, the top for underwear.

That's where I wake up almost every morning. That's where I have my first coffee and my first cigarette.

I brush my teeth, wash my face, dress, and wait to leave the house. Usually I click through the Hebrew and Arabic Israeli news sites, and sometimes I flip on the TV and passively watch the local news or the Weather Channel. It is during those mornings, from the moment I open my eyes until the moment I leave the house, that I am assailed by the sharpest pangs of longing for Palestine.

At six thirty I head out to the bus stop near the dorms. Usually I am the first passenger on the bus. I nod at the driver, whom I see almost every day, and sometimes she nods back. Off campus more passengers board — mostly gas station attendants and salespeople coming off night shifts at one of the twenty-four-hour stores. There are no college kids on the buses at that time of day and no students on their way to school.

At a quarter to seven I reach the house. I have a key and don't have to ring the bell or ask my wife's permission to enter. She's already awake, seated at the kitchen table with her coffee. Palestine drinks cappuccinos. She told me she once used to cook coffee in a pot over an open flame. When she left Tira, she turned to instant coffee, and once we could afford it she bought herself a coffee machine.

My arrival is a sign that it's time to wake the boys. Palestine no longer asks if I'd like coffee. I take my shoes off by the door, shed my winter layers, and take the wooden steps, padded with a gray American carpet, to the bedroom level. The two boys share a single room with matching beds and a desk for the eldest, who is ten. He's the one I wake first. I stroke his hair, say good morning, give him a kiss. He gets up quickly, says good morning, and gets to his feet, ready to wash his face, brush his teeth, and get dressed. Then I sit on the edge of my younger son's bed, stroke his hair, kiss his cheeks, whisper gentle words in a soft voice. He refuses to rise. He doesn't like going to kindergarten. Two years have passed and the first words out of his mouth every single day are: "I don't want to go to school." At first he said that sentence in Hebrew, but after three months in the United States he started to protest in English. The door to my daughter's room, when she's at home, is perpetually locked. She wakes up alone, wishes no one a good morning, and responds to no one when she is greeted but is always ready on time.

I head over to the garage through a side door connected to the kitchen, open the door by pressing a button, raising it a couple of feet off the ground so that the exhaust fumes don't gather inside, and start the car so that it warms up, at least slightly, while the boys slurp down the last of their cereal. Then they struggle with their shoes.

4

"It's much better for the kids," I find myself saying out loud sometimes, sitting in my student dorm after having dropped them off, now waiting for them to finish yet another day of school.

It has to be better for them, even if they don't know it yet. And they don't need to know. They're learning English, and the language will never scare them as it scares me. Even if we have to head back once the three years are up on Palestine's contract, the kids will already be using the language as if it's their own.

It would be better for them here, without a doubt. They won't have to feel humiliated, won't have to bow their heads beneath the glare of that monstrous glass ceiling. Here, so I hoped, they won't be constantly reminded that they don't belong, aren't wanted, be forced to internalize their own inferiority, compelled to weigh each word spoken in school and on the street and at work out of a fear that they might somehow upset the status of the rulers.

Even if my wife and I have to return, the kids will always have the option of fleeing to a different country, into the arms of a familiar language. The notion that they may stray far from me rises painfully to the surface every now and again. I'd like to have them nearby, always, in the same village, the same town, same neighborhood, or at least a

short drive away, along safe, orderly streets, with a safety
barrier between the lanes of oncoming traffic. Tira was an
hour from Jerusalem, and yet at times it felt so far.

The kids have never been to Tira, and my wife and I have
not been back since the wedding.

　　Ever since we met, my wife has wanted to leave the country. When she finished her doctorate at Hebrew University
she had several options for postdocs and visiting teaching
residencies at a few universities abroad, but she was forced
to turn those offers down on my account. I couched my op-
position to any move in work-related concerns — the financial
burdens of that sort of trip — but the real reason I didn't want
to go was that I knew that elsewhere it would be easier for
her to leave me. I had no doubt that moving countries would
lead to a separation between us. I hoped I could string things
along until she managed one day to love me, just as I loved her
from the moment I saw her. But her love did not materialize.
And the kids arrived and multiplied. By the time we'd left,
our daughter was eleven and already could ask questions we
couldn't answer. We had to protect her and keep her away
from Tira to the greatest possible extent.

Sometimes, when I'm left alone in the university's apartment
dorms, I click over to a local Tira site and look through
the pictures in the news articles and advertisements. I sift
through the nursery school birthday party pictures and the
sporting events and the murders, the burnt cars, the road-
works, the grand openings of the newest convenience stores

I zoom in on the photos and examine them closely, looking for familiar faces, hoping to find some of the kids who were in my class in elementary school.

I think I remember each of the forty-two kids who were with me from first to ninth grade. Many dropped out along the way and others were sent to the asfuriyya, the bird house, which is what we called the special-ed school that was founded in the village when we were in fourth grade, and to which the idiots, the blind, the impaired — those who couldn't get by — were sent. We knew nothing of special education, but we knew that whoever was sent to the asfuriyya was messed up, to be avoided, not to be played with, and if he should be found walking alone on the street then it was fine to yell at him and pelt him with tangerines. Sometimes I wonder what became of each of my forty-two classmates.

I know for a fact that one student in the class died, because I read about her on that same local news site. There was not much in the way of details in that article, no name, no cause of death, no comment from the police. The news on Tira's local site is written for the people of Tira, and they are the only ones who know to read between the lines and understand what really happened — the chain of events, the names of the suspects and their motives. The only way of knowing what's happening in Tira is to live in Tira.

Besides news sites I also look at Google Earth, at both satellite images and roads. I sit in front of the computer and move east across the globe, toward its middle, and with precise motions of my finger I approach home. Once properly positioned, I zoom in on Tira, infiltrating, from above, the streets, and, from the spot where I touch down, I navigate my way home.

I walk down the main street in our neighborhood, the way back from elementary school to home. Some of the houses have been renovated, some are newly built, old stores have been closed, and new ones have been opened in their place. The road is filled with kids dressed in the same blue uniform, backpacks on their shoulders, frozen in time as they walk with me back to their houses. The faces of the children are not clear enough to recognize and still I try to imagine their parents and I wonder if one of them was in my class. People don't leave Tira, don't abandon it. They don't have anywhere else to go. It's always the same families, same eyes, same skin color, same gaze, passed down in Tira from the war to the face-blurring cameras of Google.

I continue to stride along the main street, avoiding the dirt path that cuts away toward the cemetery. Most of the kids in the neighborhood used to take the shortcut and follow the dirt track through the graveyard, but I was scared. Even when I circled along the length of the outer wall, I'd mumble the Fatiha that my grandmother taught me to recite and that she promised would protect me from danger. I walked fast because I wanted to prove, perhaps to the neighborhood kids and perhaps to myself, that the graveyard shortcut wasn't any shorter. And actually they weren't rushing to get home, those kids from my class. They lingered in the graveyard, and I would beat them even if I took the long way at a stroll. I could hear the sounds of their laughter rolling through the cemetery wall, and I couldn't understand how they dared to laugh. Were they not taught

that laughter in a graveyard rouses the wrath of God? It took
me a while to realize that they weren't looking to shorten
the distance home; they were just looking to get rid of me.

Did they want to get rid of me because I was the kid who
reminded them of the homework we'd been given? The one
who scolded them when they talked about girls? The one
who refused to copy and refused to let others copy off him?
The one who followed the teachers' orders, never broke
the rules, and freely reminded others of what the religion
teacher had to say about the words they use, the wicked
thoughts they think, the talk of the sex they'd seen in movies and the papers?

I only realized this on the first day of junior high. I had
plotted out that day with the next-door neighbor's kid, my
best friend, who had sat next to me every day from kindergarten to the end of elementary school. In order to get over
the hump of the new experience, we ought to get to school
first, I had said, to stand in line for morning calisthenics before anyone else. And with the first indication that we may
head into class, we ought to run ahead and grab desks that
are in front of the board so that we miss nothing of what
is being taught, and we guarantee ourselves a joint desk —
together, the two of us — with no strange kids from different
neighborhoods and different schools coming between us.
When the day came, I did everything alone: I stood in line
alone, I went into class alone, I grabbed the good seats alone.
My best friend had no need to rush I told him. I'll do it all
and secure the good seats for us. If one of the kids asks to
sit next to me, at one of the two-person desks, I'll tell him

that the seat is taken and he should find himself someplace else. I remember the triumphant smile spread across my face, the giddy feeling that the plan I'd been rehearsing in my mind for weeks had succeeded. I remember the rest of the kids filing into class, most of them knowing who they wanted to sit with, snapping up the seats in pairs. And I remember the neighbor's son walking into the class, looking at me with a smile, which only subsequently felt derisive, and sitting at a different desk, alongside a different student, who had not been in our elementary school and whom I had never seen before.

I was more upset with myself than with my best friend, fuming at my blindness, my inability to see and to properly interpret the other kids' behavior. I spent three years in that junior high and was a good student. I got the best grades, didn't cheat, didn't let others cheat off me. I had no friends, nor did I not want any back then.

I kept taking the long way home, skirting the cemetery, circling around the dead. I walked around the graves of my maternal grandfather, my paternal grandmother, my two uncles, and my young cousin. My paternal grandfather was buried elsewhere, in the village in which he was born and killed, where there was a graveyard that is no longer. Twice a year, when we visited the cemetery all together, on Eid al-Fitr and Eid al-Adha, the graveyard was thronged with visitors and I was still afraid. My grandmother, who read the fear in my eyes, would say in a tone of wonder: "You're scared of the dead? They aren't scary at all. It's the living you should be afraid of."

On the computer I advanced through the streets until I arrived at my house and saw a car parked out front. That was surely my father's car. I was so happy and I hoped that he was awake, because I didn't want to have to wait to show him my perfect score in math. I tried to enter the house, prying my fingers apart on the touch pad, but I couldn't go beyond the porch and the front door. I almost yelled out: "Dad," "Mom." But no door was opened.

5

When I pick up my kids from school I try to read the expressions on their faces. Are they happy? Are they glad to see me? Did they wait all day long till the moment that they were allowed to go home, as I had done at their age? And do they have friends here? After all, we've been in the States for two years and they've never once invited a friend to their house or been invited to the home of one of their classmates. "Yes," they always say in answer to my questions and never offer further details. I had hoped things would be different here.

At night, after the boys have gone to sleep, I leave the house. Only rarely does my wife ask me to stay. She'll say she's afraid and maybe suggest having a glass of wine. And then we sleep together, and afterward I retreat to the downstairs couch for some shut-eye. But usually, once the two boys are bathed and in bed and have fallen asleep, I check to see that they're breathing and then I bundle up and take the bus back to the student dorms.

The bus goes through the center of town, and I watch the people in the few bars and restaurants clustered between the city building and the train station. Sometimes I toy with the idea of getting off the bus and having a few pints of beer before continuing on my way. I did that a few times during our first few months here, but soon enough I realized that I wouldn't have a regular hangout here as I'd hoped. The bartenders are very polite, but other than asking if they can get you anything, they don't speak to the customers—at least not the foreign ones. It seems to me that the locals know one another, smile at each other, and ask, "How are you this evening?" But they never really intend on having a conversation.

Sometimes I imagine myself stepping off the bus with ease, full of self-confidence. I saw a show on TV here with an expert who explained that one needn't be particularly good-looking or rich when trying to pick up a woman at a bar, but that instead it was all about self-confidence and the way it's broadcast in body language, facial expressions, and gazes. "How are you doing this evening, ma'am?" I imagine myself asking the young lady on the seat beside me. She will find out the truth soon enough, but by then she'll want me specifically for my lack of confidence and gloominess, my lonesomeness and longing. She'll confide in me that she can't stand all those überconfident dudes and that she, too, is a bit lost, and it's not entirely clear to her what she wants out of life. She'll be local and she'll teach me the local mores, slowly revealing all of the city's hidden treasures, the secrets that no foreigner has been exposed to. I'll know where to get the best food, where the best music is being played, the hidden spots that people like us hang out in. She'll help me improve my English and after a few weeks of hesitancy, she'll no longer be bashful and will start on my accent. I'll be her lover from a distant land, the one who will teach her about worlds she's only heard about on the news. We'll harbor a shared pain over our unspoken acknowledgement that nothing will come of this relationship, since we belong to different worlds, and the future is so uncertain. It will be a temporary and impossible relationship that will suit both of us at this stage of our lives. Knowing that it's not forever, we'll love each other passionately, until she realizes what it is she wants to do with her life—and until I am forgiven by Palestine.

In Jerusalem I had a regular watering hole, and when I look out the window of the bus on the way to the apartment dorms, at the yellow lights of the local bars, I see it. I first went there at the age of twenty-one, just as I was starting to publish articles in the local papers as a freelancer. I joined a crew of veteran reporters, who were in the habit of parting with the workweek over a few rounds of drinks, a pause before moving on to new topics and new articles.

We would meet up at eleven at night and we'd head home just as the delivery boys started their routes, so that we'd hit the doorstep after the newspaper had. I couldn't get into bed until I'd looked it over, found my articles, made sure the heads and subheads were right, the pictures perfect. First, I'd look and see if the article had a reefer on the front page and then the page number and the amount of real estate that the piece had been given. I couldn't hope for any better weekends than when my name was scrawled on the front page, proof that I'd done a good job, a sort of appreciation for labor performed in a field in which the pay was never a real draw.

None of those veterans, besides me, stayed on for long at the paper and none continued coming to the bar, which

changed ownerships and names. At times I'd see them reporting from the field or commentating in the TV news
studios, occasionally finding their bylines in the national
newspapers. Those who left journalism became politicians
and advisers. I became the oldest staff reporter in the newsroom of the local paper, which, in the age of internet and
satellite TV, had lost all of its luster. At the bar, too, I was
the oldest of the regulars.

Eventually the paper became a freebie that Jerusa-
lemites consented to take home mostly for the ads and the
coupons provided by local businesses. When I started working there our offices were in the center of town, a few feet
from Zion Square. By the time I left, the offices had moved
to an industrial area south of the city, the paper surrounded
by garages, workshops, and small businesses. There was no
longer a need for many reporters and so the office space was
slashed, too. Email enabled reporters to work from home,
so there was no need for a newsroom or computer desks
for the few remaining reporters. The digital camera made
the darkroom redundant, and the graphics programs on the
computers made the editing room unnecessary.

The paper, which was once full of life and packed with
journalists who thought they'd change the world, was, over
the years, drained of content, and the advertising section
swelled as the newsroom shrank. It was then that I was
offered the position of editor in chief. There was no pay
raise offered with the job, but the publisher knew I'd take
the offer because I had nowhere else to go. The young reporters, mostly journalism majors who thought it would
be a good stepping-stone on the path to TV fame, were
drafted personally by the publisher. Every now and again

I'd discover that the education reporter was the daughter of the owner of some famous hotel in the city or that the town hall reporter was a communications major whose uncle was the owner of a wedding hall that recently bought two pairs of ongoing full-page ads in the paper. My role as editor was simply to paginate and to make order among the weak roll of articles, most of which were simply copied from PR firms' press releases.

On Thursday nights I'd put the paper to bed, send the files to Tel Aviv for printing, and head out to have my weekly beers alone at the usual bar, which I made sure to leave before eleven, because who even goes out before then?

6

That night, four years before we left the country, after putting the paper to bed, I had four pints of Goldstar and a shot of Jameson. That was the usual lineup during those days. I knew that if I was caught driving I'd lose my license, but I continued taking the car from the newsroom to a parking lot near the bar in the center of town and was never stopped or caught on the way home. Word was that the police were set up with breathalyzers and such only on Friday and Saturday nights, when the kids went out to party, and I knew that the chances of them stopping someone my age with a car seat in the back were slim. And yet, that night, right after starting up the car, still trying to navigate my way out of the parking spot, I was blinded by headlights.

"License and registration, please," a man in uniform and an Arabic accent said.

I handed over the papers and added a tfadal and a smile, hoping that Arab solidarity would foster a certain leniency. Later on, I learned from the police report that he was a volunteer from East Jerusalem. He asked me to exhale into this plastic contraption and then had me switch off the ignition and hand him the keys. Speaking to me in his broken Hebrew, he asked that I accompany him to the car around the corner and said that this was just an initial test, an indication, and that I'd have to undergo a more serious examination, which would officially determine if I was guilty of drinking and driving. He passed me on to a different police officer, also an Arab. I could tell that he was from one of the villages in the Galilee, but I couldn't tell if he was Druze, Christian, or Muslim. It was a clear and cold Jerusalem night and after a long battery of tests I felt like I was going to freeze. The Druze/Christian/Muslim cop was dressed warmly in a police jacket. He spoke to me solely in Hebrew, which was better than the volunteer's, and I responded in Arabic. I asked him to do me a favor, told him that I was the editor of a local Jerusalem paper, a father to young children, but he said there was nothing he could do once the breathalyzer results showed a very high blood alcohol content. After filling out the forms, he took my license, gave me back the keys, and handed me a sheath of paperwork, informing me that I had to report to the desk officer at the central police precinct the following morning.

The officer on duty the next day was a Jew. He told me, after looking at my license: "Come back for it in thirty days." Then he served me with a summons to traffic court in Givat Shaul. "You ought to get a lawyer," he said, noting that he had to impound the vehicle for at least thirty days, but he asked, nonetheless, "Is there a reason you can state why I should, perhaps, not impound the car?"

I told the officer that I have children and that my wife works at the university, and it's the only car we have. He handed back the keys, told me I could drive the car home, that he would give me half an hour before the license suspension went into effect but that if I was caught on the road afterward it would mean immediate arrest. I thanked him.

I hired a lawyer, who called me back two months later to tell me that he'd reached a deal with the prosecution: an eleven-month suspension, a two-thousand-shekel fine, and sixty hours of community service.

Several days later I deposited my license with the court, paid the fine at the postal bank, and presented myself to the probation officer, who would decide on the nature of the community service. In a conversation with the officer I told him that I was the editor of a newspaper, that I'd studied literature in college, and that I don't know how to do a thing besides write and edit. He asked if I know how to tell a story, and I said yes, even though the only story I'd ever had published was less than one page long and had been printed in a college magazine many years before.

"In Hebrew or Arabic?" the officer inquired.

"Hebrew," I responded.

He shuffled through my papers and then asked if I'd like to volunteer at an old-age home in Jerusalem, even though it was not a suggestion or a form of volunteerism.

He gave me the number of the home's culture and entertainment coordinator, Batya, and said I should be in touch with her. "She'll be in charge of you," the officer said, adding that she'll be the one to sign off on the hours I've put in, ensuring that I complete the sixty hours of obligatory community service as stipulated in the plea bargain agreement.

Batya said she was very happy that I'd decided to volunteer at the Founders Home, a top-notch establishment that offers its residents an array of cultural enrichment opportunities. She said that they have been looking for a while now for someone to teach creative writing classes to the residents. She suggested an hour a week, and I said that an hour is too short for a writing class and suggested two hours, mostly because I wanted to pay my dues and be done with the punishment as soon as possible.

We settled on Sunday, the quietest day at the paper, at four in the afternoon, so that the residents would have enough time to get organized for dinner once class was dismissed. That is how I found my first clients: the writing class drew much interest but very little willingness to write. Mostly the residents wanted to tell me things that seemed unique or worthy and hoped that I would write these vignettes down for them. Others would write a few lines, read them aloud, and then crumple the paper and continue the story aloud. All of them felt that they had memories that were unique and rare, and they all wanted to see their stories in print.

Some of the residents came to the writing workshop with books in which they were mentioned or quoted, books that memorialized the founding of certain kibbutzim or moshavim or books published by the history presses of the Yad Vashem World Holocaust Remembrance Center or the Ministry of Defense, which were considered the most prestigious. The residents whose names were mentioned in those pages were very proud indeed, even if the mention came only in the form of small print in the bibliography, in which, say, the names of an entire company were written out.

I wrote the life stories of those who were not featured in any book, those who felt wronged by omission, those whose stories were remarkably similar to the others, covering the same well-trod ground of suffering and adversity and, in its wake, revival and success. All of them felt heroic and victimized, no less so than the heroes and victims immortalized in the official memorial books.

During the first few weeks of community service a resident approached me and introduced himself as a former fighter in the pre-state Palmach militia and said that if I were to hear the stories he had to tell, "Well, then," I'd realize that this was material that had yet to be put to paper, and if it were to be, it was guaranteed to be a bestseller. He had always wanted to tell the story of his life but had never had the time. For the stories that are unfurled in the memoir *1948*, with all due respect to Yoram Kaniuk, whom he hadn't read but who, he knew, had hardly taken part in the decisive battles of the war and, well, if he wrote the way he shot then he really was in a bad way, amounted to naught when compared to the tales he had to tell. The former militiaman offered to pay me for the writing of his memoir, and a week later I started recording him talking about the dangers facing the fragile Jewish settlement in the pre-state days and the spirit of heroism among the young fighters in the face of Arab hostility and banditry. He promised to keep the arrangement between us a secret, but apparently he did no such thing, because, within days, I was asked by the daughter of one of the residents, a native of Baghdad, if I would consider writing his, too, which was, in her opinion, no less fascinating and centered on his immigration to Israel. Her father, she said, was a humble and bashful man, but his children have always felt that his story is worthy of professional documentation and distribution and that now, with him in an old-age home and time being something he had in abundance, he had been persuaded to work with me on a memoir so that the grandchildren and the great-grandchildren will know from whence they've come and have a sense of the hardships endured by their forebears in order to bequeath them this land.

I didn't do much in the way of editing those first two life accounts, aside from keeping the chronology in order and underscoring the tales that seemed most important to the clients. I didn't yet dare tinker with the childhoods of the protagonists, didn't yet edit their memories. I wrote, as I'd been tasked, about the Palmach militiamen and about Baghdad, about riches that had been abandoned and riots that had menaced, the trials of immigration, acclimatization, and success. I did not ask these first clients about their earliest memory or about what they tell themselves before shutting their eyes at night. Those habits started with the third book, which was also commissioned by one of the participants in the workshop, after our final class, once I no longer owed the Founders Home anything. This client didn't want her own life story transcribed but rather that of her son, who had fallen during a war. She handed me photos—some in black and white and some in color—and asked that I incorporate them into the narrative. She said that she would cover the costs of printing the book and that ten copies would suffice, and she told me about her son, as she remembered him. At one point she said, she could recall every single day spent with her son. But now she had started to forget—and she was terrified that if she forgot everything, her son would truly and terminally be dead.

She told me all she could remember, and yet the cassette was hardly filled. Mostly she recalled her son when he was little, before he was drafted. The events that led to his death were familiar to her only from the reports on the radio and the TV.

Upon her request, I wrote about her dead son in rhyming verse, gleaning inspiration from the photos, from what appeared to be his delicate demeanor, even when he was in uniform and armed with a rifle. It was a short book, like a children's book, with pictures of her son from one to twenty-one accompanied by poems that described his mother's memories and, for the first time, those that I invented.

I gave him a childhood love, whom I called Merav, a beautiful and bashful girl. And in this book, Merav insisted that her name be written with no *i*. And she would get angry when people were confused about that, but the son never made that sort of mistake, though he insisted on calling her Meiravi, "with a bunch of *i*'s."

He had a wonderful smile that all of his friends recalled.

He flashed that smile in one of the poems, which described the day he fell off the swing in kindergarten, and his father came toward him with a handkerchief, and he didn't even notice that his father had been behind him talking to the kindergarten teacher.

And that was the exact smile he flashed when he fell in battle, and when his mother read it she said that in truth — although she hadn't been allowed to see the body — she knew that he had died with that same smile on his face.

Peacefully, fearlessly, with the smile she remembered, just as in the book.

7

Now I'm alone in the student dorms with my recorder, wishing for a different story to tell, one that isn't this one, which might be my father's or might be mine.

My father never hired me as his ghostwriter. He didn't want me documenting his life and had no desire to leave a legacy for later generations. It is I who insists on re-creating a story that no one asked me to re-create, in the pages of a book that will never be written. After all, it's been two months since I started and I haven't written a single word. It's been two months and I don't even know what language I'll write in or who the protagonist is.

Over the past two months I've gone back and looked through the life stories saved on my computer. The full and unadulterated transcripts were saved separately from the one which I would start as a new file and begin editing. After my initial edit, I'd click on Track Changes and document the deletions, comments, and additions I made to the original life story. At the end of the process I'd send the clients a clean document, in which there was no indication of what had been altered in their life story.

A good editor, I learned at the paper, is one who can rewrite, reorder, delete, and add—without the reporter noticing the changes once the article's been published. He will believe, surely and truly, that he authored every single word on the page.

During my first year as a ghostwriter of memoirs I managed to double my annual income. True, documenting the lives of others left little time for my own life, but the work meant that for the first time I felt we could actually shoulder the burden of a mortgage, and I tried in vain to convince Palestine to buy a house together and to have it listed in both of our names, instead of the short-term rentals we'd lived in for all of those years.

I wrote thirty books over the next four years — or at least bound collections of pages that looked like books. My asking price was ten thousand shekels per hundred pages, with an average of around 150 words per page. Big font, double space, wide margins. The formatting never bothered those who were listed as the authors and they loved the fact that their life stories, or those of their loved ones, appeared thick and voluminous. Most of the clients chose to have the book professionally produced, which included cover design, layout, copyediting, and printing. All of them wanted to insert photos. The standard deal was ten black-and-white photos on regular paper in the middle of the book for one thousand shekels. Color doubled the price. Other than the printing and the binding, which were done at a press in the industrial zone in Givat Shaul, I did everything myself: the design and the copyediting and the proofreading. When designing the cover, I used a picture provided by the client or his or her family and spent less than half an hour seated before a software program that one of the graphic designers at the paper recommended, reading through the tutorial that more than sufficed for my purposes.

❊   ❊   ❊

Thirty books, the last of which I submitted to the printing press two weeks before our departure from Jerusalem. I left a mailing address with the printing press secretary, who was the daughter of the owner, for a shipment of thirty copies. My final client was a retired Tel Aviv–Jaffa municipal worker, whose memoir was paid for by the city as part of his severance package, in honor of the city's one hundredth birthday. The idea was to help assemble the memoirs of the municipal workers born before, or with, the founding of the state, in 1948. Ten books featuring the stories of ten different Jews were set to be published. But the city is home to a sizable Arab population as well, and one of the councilmen, a representative from Jaffa, demanded that the Arab retirees not be discriminated against and that if they met the standards for the memoir bonus and their memories served, then they, too, were entitled to a book written in their name.

Long after the centennial had passed I got a call from city hall in Tel Aviv asking if, in fact, I ghostwrite memoirs, as it says on my website, Stories of Youth, which I set up in order to help spread the word once the business got going. "Our team here at Stories of Youth is skilled in both Hebrew and Arabic," I'd noted, among other things.

The client, who was born in 1940, had been a sanitation worker in Jaffa. He wasn't even from Jaffa, and he didn't want to give any information about his life but, approached by city hall, he agreed, concerned that refusal could jeopardize his pension. The worker and his family were originally from the village of Irtakh, up on the ridge in the northern West Bank, near Tulkarm, and had left the village on account of a blood feud in which one of his family members had been involved, forcing them to move to a tiny room in one of the orchards owned by a wealthy Jaffa family. When the war broke out and Jaffa was emptied of its residents, the sanitation worker's father decided to move into his employee's home, the owner of the orchard, and there they stayed until, after the war, the municipality forced them to move to one of the housing projects in which they live to this day. They left out of fear that the authorities would discover that they were not the true owners. "But none of this is to be written, my son," the worker said during our interview, and though I transcribed everything he said, including the request to not document this chapter of his life, I didn't include it in the finished memoir.

What is your first memory?

What do you mean?

What's your first memory of childhood?

What makes you think I'm dealing with memories?

Everyone has memories.

Sometimes the hardships of life leave no time for memories.

And yet the old worker told of how he remembered the British soldiers stopping his family en route from Irtakh to Jaffa. He was the oldest of five siblings, three boys and two girls. He remembered his terror, the soldiers' fingers curled around their triggers, and the way his father told them in Arabic they didn't speak — seasoned with English words like "mister" and "please, sir" — that he had to get to the new job his cousin had arranged for him near Lod. The soldiers demanded to know what was in the donkey cart and the jugs. He also remembered the look in his mother's eyes, the fear that the English, who were known to like goat's cheese, would discover that she had stored a dry cheese in one of the jugs, the only food for the family until God delivered an answer to their plight. The soldier pointed to the jug with the cheese and asked, "What do you have in there, water? I'm thirsty. Give me a drink."

The mother said, "There was water, but it's gone." And then, before the soldier approached the jug, she placed her open hand over it and in a quick movement turned it upside down, palming the cheese inside and telling the soldier: "You see, there is no water. It's finished," and the Englishman gave up and let them go on their way, and the worker looked back for the last time upon the village in which he was born and saw nothing.

The old laborer let me include the story about the British soldiers once I convinced him that the British had long since left. But I did not document the blood feud or the village of his birth. The sanitation worker insisted that I write how good it was when the Jews came, how everything got so much better, praise be to God, and how his father found work and received medical treatment from the state in his old age. And write how much easier everything became, with running water and electricity, and thank God, write how well I was treated by the municipality and how for forty years I worked alongside Jews who were like brothers to me, like brothers I tell you. And thank God, what more does a man need aside from raising children, sending them to school, watching them grow and becoming adults and starting families of their own. And write that in '48 the Arabs conspired against the Jews and that their leaders asked that they step out for two days at most and that after

that the Arab armies would come and butcher the Jews and
then the residents of Jaffa would be free to return to their
homes and to live in tranquility. He never actually heard
any such sentence from an Arab leader or from a resident
of Jaffa, but include it, he said. Do me a favor. The book is
in Hebrew anyway, and no resident of Jaffa will ever read
it. Write what they want to hear and may the Lord light
your path.

I erased whatever the municipal worker wanted me to
erase. And I wrote about his poverty-stricken life among
the orchards, of hunger and locusts, and of how his parents
would collect the manure left behind by the horses that
sauntered down the orchard paths and that once the droppings were dry they would rub them between their hands,
foraging for grains of wheat and kernels of corn, saving the
barley for kindling. And how Israel saved them from a life
of poverty and the shame of hunger.

When I sent him the final text for authorization he
didn't even respond, and when I called him he said the book
was excellent, thank you very much, may your hands be
safeguarded for the service you've provided. Maybe his
children had read the book and maybe his grandchildren,
and perhaps they took pleasure in the fictitious scenes of
familial warmth that I added to their grandfather's recollections. How the little nook was cozy even in the harshest
of winter days and how his mother, who had tricked the
British soldiers, would tell, even though she couldn't read
or write, bedtime stories and legends to her small children,
sending them off to sleep full of hope. And though in real-
ity the worker had said little about his wife beyond may

Allah have mercy on her and that she was a good woman, I added some words of love when I described his parting with her, and how, ever since her passing, he still whispers good night to her as though she were beside him in bed. When I described her funeral, I wrote that the sanitation worker's wife lay in the casket with a delicate smile upon her face, the same life-affirming, girly smile she wore when he first met her, and I described how he kissed her goodbye on the forehead, as my father had done to my dead grandmother, speaking the very words I had heard my father whisper to his mother: "Ma'a as-salameh, mama, ma'a as-salameh, my dear."

8

Other than the sanitation worker I had only one other Arab client. He was a former Member of Knesset, a representative of a left-wing Jewish party, whose voice I recognized when he called me to ask about the services I provide and who may have hired me simply on account of an honorific I used during our call that he seemed to think was either evidence of a deep appreciation for his public service or my belonging to a family clan that supported the party. The MK wanted to have his life story written in Hebrew, and, unlike the rest of my clients who generally made do with two to three dozen copies for friends and family, he aspired to have the book accepted by a commercial publishing house. The Arab MK said that the senior publishing executives he'd spoken with had assured him that when the final manuscript was ready they would be happy to have a look. He was already over the age of eighty and had not written a word about his life, and all he wanted of me was to get the story down on the page.

Our first meeting was at his house in lower Galilee. He greeted me in a blue suit and red tie and led me to a sort of reception area, outfitted with dozens of couches and tables, a relic of his days as a politician, when he was often asked to receive ministers and prime ministers and other distinguished guests. Framed photographs of varying sizes covered the walls, featuring the MK with Israeli statesmen, foreign leaders, and diplomats — Yasser Arafat, King Hussein, and Hosni Mubarak.

The MK sat, in what I suspected was his usual spot, on a large couch bookended by two other couches. Before him was a long, low table. He asked what I'd like to drink, and I said water would be fine. "Just water?" he asked and laughed when I grabbed one of the bottles from the table. When his wife entered, in a long and impressive dress, as though she were going to a wedding or a formal event, he asked her to make coffee for both of us and asked how I take mine. "Black, please," I said to the woman who appeared to be at least a full decade younger than the MK.

Two to three meetings always sufficed with other clients but with the MK I had to conduct five separate interviews, and he always greeted me in the same reception hall, in a suit I hadn't yet seen, his wife clad in a formal dress, the colors of which changed with each meeting. The coffee was always the same, served in porcelain cups covered with decorative flowers.

"I'll speak in Hebrew," he declared during our first meeting. "You're writing in Hebrew and so it will surely be easier for you to record this way." I knew that he thought that his Hebrew was superior to mine and that he'd like his diplomatic eloquence, which he'd acquired during the long years of addressing the Jewish public — fellow politicians, voters, and readers — to serve him one last time while recounting the stations of his life.

The former MK spoke like a politician when discussing his personal life. His depictions strove to highlight his most dear and yet not very significant achievements, underscoring his virtues at every turn. He told of how he had joined the ranks of the Labor Party in the sixties at Hebrew University and how he had believed then, as now, that Arab-Jewish cooperation as based on the shared values of coexistence, liberty, and democracy will bring prosperity for Jews and Arabs alike. He spoke of the disappointment he felt in recent years, as his party was losing its hold on the rudders of power, and he expressed concern for the future of the region and of Arab-Jewish relations, which he viewed as being pushed to ever lower depths of segregation and polarization. He spoke in Hebrew because he knew that the only hope he had of marketing the book was among Jews of his age group and not Arabs who certainly had no interest in hearing what he had to say. And yet it seemed to me that nonetheless, even in Hebrew, the MK strove to detail his efforts for an Arab readership, telling of how teachers, principals, and Arab school supervisors would show up at his office and how he helped the local councils and the school systems and how the upper echelons of Arab society, the communists and nationalists alike, arrive at his office and fill his ample reception room. He sought to relay tales of how he would, often in the small hours of the night, assist families who had lost loved ones abroad and had come to him for guidance and assistance in how to bring the body home for burial. And the efforts he would make in trying to help concerned parents secure the release of loved ones who had been arrested at rallies or while engaged in political activity. His recollections seemed to be an indictment of the Arabs, who had forgotten his contribution and treated him instead like a sort of traitor because he had joined the ranks of a Zionist party. "And what did their heroes in Knesset do other than make noise and cause a spectacle?" he asked, his voice filled with an uncharacteristic anger. "Did they connect any villages to the electrical grid? To the national water carrier? The phone company? Did they inject money into the school system? Did they deliver sewage systems to their towns? No. They did nothing besides talk. Everyone knows this and everyone stays silent. But I would prefer, of course, that you not quote the last two sentences."

In the book I wrote that the MK, who had been abandoned by his constituency, switched into Arabic when I asked him about his childhood memories. At first he spoke in the sentences he had learned to recite, a historic recounting of events as they've been written and revised and shaped over the years, about '48 and the "rescue" army of Arab regulars that arrived in the village of his birth. He spoke of the signing of the 1949 Armistice Agreements, the arrival of the Jewish soldiers and the collection of weapons from the residents, the transformation of the town into a part of Israel. I asked him to describe his parents' home for me. And when he asked, "What good will that do?" I encouraged him to trust me and promised that if he wasn't satisfied with the end product those passages could of course be excised from the book. In Hebrew he started describing how his parents had a simple home, of straw bale and mortar, like the rest of the houses in the neighborhood, with his family on one floor—six brothers and three sisters—and the farm animals: a donkey and two cows, which were brought inside on cold nights.

He described how his father was capable of reading a newspaper, but his mother was illiterate, as were most of the women in the village. Still in Hebrew, he apologized for his childhood and insisted on noting that with time his parents had built a proper stone house.

I asked the MK about the war in Arabic, and he responded in kind, not noticing that we'd shifted languages and didn't, as I wrote, say anything about the feeling of humiliation or the fear that seized him when he accompanied his father, along with the rest of the men, to the village school and didn't talk about being certain that he would never see him again, because he had heard talk of the atrocities done by the Jews. He didn't mention that his mother cried, regretting not having left with those who fled, and what worth is there to family honor when there is no husband, and what worth is there to courage when life is severed. But his father returned in the evening, and the MK, who was a child then, was delighted, and he recalled wanting to hug his father, even though such behavior was not permitted, for he was already six, a boy old enough to start acting like a man. Without words he told of the silence of his father, who was not joyous like the rest of the family upon his safe return, and his father said not a word and did not draw the kids in to his embrace as one might expect of someone saved from the jaws of death. It was in that moment that for the first time he knew the meaning of humiliation, though he did not have the language to describe the feeling, knowing only that the vanquished face of his father would not dim in his memory until he got older and learned to interpret glances and give words to the expressions of the senses. He did not need words, however, to vow that he would avenge in some way what the Jews had done to his father's gaze, but he possessed neither the strength nor the courage to follow through.

While editing his childhood years I was more concerned by his possible reaction than with my other clients. At first I made the decision to stick to his words and phrases, adhering to the stories he told, but I wasn't able to control myself, and in the chapter that describes his life in Jerusalem and his initial acquaintance with Israeli students I described the difficulty he faced with the language and the foreign culture and the fear of falling from the path of the just and the concern that if he adopted their language and their ways he would never be able to return home. I told of his pride in the face of their racism and sense of superiority, which his democracy-loving friends tried in vain to hide, and how they were incapable of veiling, even if they did try, the tone of superiority that wormed into every comment and conversation.

In the opening chapter of his childhood I added sentences in Arabic that he never said. I told his future readers: "There are memories that are feelings, which cannot be expressed in any way but through body language or in the mother tongue, in the dialect and the accent and the cadence that cannot be re-created in a foreign language and perhaps not in the original, either. And therefore I shall write the following chapter in Arabic." And I wrote a childhood story that the Member of Knesset never told. I told of the humiliation that he saw in his father's eyes, even though all he said was that all of the men had been convened for a "meeting" in the school, a meeting in which the new rulers detailed the new rules. The MK did not protest, not over the Arabic that I put on his tongue and not the vow of revenge that I had him swear and not fulfill.

I never saw the MK's book in stores, and I saw nothing about it in the papers. When I submitted the final manuscript, he paid me the remainder of my fee as we'd agreed upon and had me sign a document prepared by one of his children, whom I'd never met but was clearly a lawyer, stipulating that I had no rights or claims to the manuscript, along with a few more lines of legalese ensuring that I could not steal the MK's life story. Two days after I submitted the book he called me to thank me for the wonderful work and told me that he had sent copies to several publishing houses and is convinced he will be hearing from them shortly and then he will decide which house will be the right one for his autobiography. He said nothing about the memories I had added.

Six months after leaving Jerusalem and moving to Illinois, I returned to the edited copy of his book, to the version marked up with Track Changes, and I went over the deletions and additions. I did that every now and again: even after the books had been sent to the presses and printed up, I continued to rework the lives, as saved in the memory of my computer.

Sometimes, as I reread, I regretted having donated pleasant childhood memories of mine to the stories of different clients, and at times I would read the versions of the edited files, take the cursor and put it over a memory I had added and choose the Reject Change icon, reclaiming the memory as my own. But it was too late. The final draft had already been sent to the clients and printed. The memory had become theirs and would never again be mine.

One day after looking through the MK's altered childhood memories, I found a short article on a Hebrew news site announcing that the former Member of Knesset had passed away. There was no picture and no mention of a memoir; no one eulogized him and no one left any comments.

C

1

When I was a kid, the houses in the old immigrant neighborhood of Kfar Saba, a ten-minute walk from Meir Hospital,
used to remind me of the houses in Tira. They didn't look
like the houses of the Jews, and those few that did have red-
tile roofs seemed out of place, like the first red-tile homes
in Tira had done in the eighties. "Bayt Karamid," we'd say
when we wanted to note the lavishness of a new house in
the village—"a house with tiles"—even though those tiles
generally just slanted over a balcony or were tented over a
set of stairs leading to the front door.

"The Jews are confused," my father used to say in the
face of our excitement about the tiles. "Tiles are for snow. It
never snows here, so why would we need tiles. All you get
from having them are pigeons and their droppings." And
yet, when it came time to draw houses, nearly every single
one of the kids in my elementary school class drew them
with red-tile roofs. We never drew houses that resembled
the houses in which we lived.

I pushed open the creaking metal gate on HaRav Kook
Street and walked down the tiled path to a two-story house
with peeling paint and exposed sections of gray cement. It
was the sort of house that was built in a rush during the

fifties, in the face of mass immigration, the sort of house about which my father would say when we drove through Kfar Saba: "This is where they put the Yemenites." He would call the Aliya neighborhood, named for the act of Jewish immigration to Israel, the Alia Neighborhood and until a rather late age I thought it was named after an Arab woman, like Queen Alia of Jordan, since the Yemenites must have been Arabs.

It was close to eight in the morning when I called the landlady from the public phone in the hospital. "Hallo," came the alert voice of an elderly woman, and I apologized for the early hour and told her that I had rented out the room over the internet and that I knew check-in was only in the afternoon, but I'd landed not long ago after a twenty-four-hour journey, and I wanted to see if, perhaps, I could arrive earlier.

"Of course, honey, we're waiting for you," the woman said. "Come whenever you like. I'm at home. You have the address, right?"

"Yes," I replied. "I have it, thank you so much, really."

My mother had arrived at the hospital at seven that morning accompanied by my little brother Mahmoud, who shook my hand hesitantly. Hamouda, we called him, and he was fifteen when I saw him last; now he's twenty-nine, a father to a two-year-old girl and a nurse at a psychiatric hospital on the outskirts of Tel Aviv. I wanted to hug him, my little brother, even though he no longer looked like the clumsy adolescent who I missed so dearly and only the bashful smile and the lowered eyes resembled the picture I had stored in my head.

My father remained asleep. I told them that he had woken up and asked for water and that he had said a few words, that his urine bag had filled toward morning and that the nurse had said that there's a marked improvement in his condition and that there was no longer a need for oxygen. He's still fatigued from the anesthesia and the pills and he should be allowed to recuperate and to awake in his own good time. "No visitors," the Russian nurse, who finished her shift at 7:00 a.m., said. "Just immediate family and no more than two in the room at the same time. Preferably just one."

"Alhamdulillah," my mother said, praising God. Her hair was covered with a kerchief, and I couldn't tell if she had become religious and when this may have happened. Was my father now also a believer?

"Have you had anything to eat?" she asked, as though I were a schoolboy just now back from studies.

"Yes," I lied. "I ate in the café downstairs. A sandwich with feta cheese."

"You have to come home," she whispered, crying and nearly hugging me. "You must be dead tired. Go home, my son, go, take a shower, rest, sleep, have something to eat. There isn't much in the house, but there's fresh bread and labaneh and some salami in the fridge. Go home. I fixed up your bed, put new sheets on. Don't be afraid, nothing will happen to you. I swear to you, nothing. Everything's good. Everything's okay. The village has changed. Everyone has their own troubles. No one's interested in other people's affairs. In the name of Allah, my sweet, go rest, go home, my son."

"I can give you a ride," my younger brother said and checked the time on his cell phone. "I've got time before my shift starts."

"Thanks," I replied. "It's okay, though. I'm going to stay here a bit longer and then I'll get a share taxi to Tira."

"You sure?"

"A hundred percent," I told him, and he clasped Dad's hand for a second, checked the data on his graph, said he'd be back after his shift at the hospital, and made Mom swear that she'd update him about even the slightest change in his condition.

"Your father was afraid of dying without seeing you again," my mother said once my brother left. "He would say that all the time." I wanted to ask why, in that case, he never asked to see me during all those years and why she, my mother, never called to ask how I was doing.

"You have no shame," she said. "You have no heart. We don't even know your children. You prevented us from seeing our own grandchildren." She dabbed her eyes with a handkerchief and only then did I notice how old she'd gotten. Wrinkles crowned her forehead and creased her neck, covering the backs of her hands and skin at her wrists.

And maybe she really did want me to come back. Maybe she did ask to see me, inquire whether I had kids, the kids that I told my father about for the first time in a message shortly before boarding the flight to America. Maybe for fourteen years she begged and cried about not being able to endure the distance between her and her son, the longing lashing at her heart, and maybe it was my father who stood like a wall between us. She wasn't afraid of him — that I always knew — but she loved him truly and fully and surely didn't want her actions to cause him sorrow. At times I thought that my mother was the one who convinced my father to do the right thing, banishing me, chasing away the shame before it stuck to them for eternity, to all their children, tarnishing their names and ruining the future that she sought for them all. And maybe, I tried convincing myself, she preferred the pain of separation and distance simply because she knew it was in my best interest. Maybe she knew, like me, that any link to them and to Tira would only cause suffering to me and my wife, more severe even than that which accompanied the beginning of our relationship. My mother and father, like my wife and I, knew that there was nowhere for us to return to and that nothing would ever be restored to the way it was.

"Enough, Mom," I said to her and for the first time since we met up yesterday I touched her shoulder and led her to the couch beneath the ICU window. "Please, don't cry."

"But now you are going home," she stated determinedly, and I looked at my father, as though waiting for him to authorize the request. But he just lay there with his eyes shut, his face covered in two-day-old stubble, like the stubble he hadn't shaved when my grandmother, his mother, died.

"Okay," I told my mother, feeling smothered and wanting only to leave the ICU room. "How long will you be here?"

"All day, till night, I suppose." She fished around inside her handbag and produced a key, the same key I remembered, only the key ring had changed, and it now was in the shape of a plastic square framing the Surat al-Fatihah. I tucked it into my pocket.

"Do not fear, my son," she said. "No one remembers you anymore."

2

I knocked weakly on the front door of the house on HaRav Kook Street in the Aliya neighborhood. The family name, Hadad, was etched at eye level into a slab of eucalyptus wood. I strained my ears, hoping to catch the sound of footsteps, confirming that my soft knocking had been heard by the old lady who had answered the phone fifteen minutes earlier. There was a bell hanging on the right side of the doorframe, but on account of the early hour and the chance that some members of the household may still be sleeping, I preferred not to ring it.

"Shalom," Miriam said, introducing herself and smiling. She was younger than I'd expected, perhaps sixty, though I have never been able to guess people's ages. "Are you Saeed?" she asked.

"Yes," I replied, and I was ready to answer all of the questions I suspected she might ask. Yes, I'm an Arab, and I am currently living in the United States with my wife and kids. My wife has a job there, a faculty position at one of the state universities, and I just got an emergency call from the family saying that my father's in a life-threatening situation, so I got on the first flight I could and came to visit him here at Meir Hospital. Lung cancer, and yes, he's okay, thank you. Where am I from? I won't say Tira, because it makes no sense that a son of the village, situated a two-minute drive from the tenements, would choose to pay 150 shekels a night for a room that serves only one purpose, housing those who live far away and have loved ones in the hospital nearby. I'll say I'm from up north and won't have an answer when she asks, "So, why is your dad being treated here?" For there are perfectly respectable hospitals up north and Meir is not the sort of place that people go out of their way to get to, preferring it over more proximate hospitals.

But Miriam only said, "Welcome, Saeed. Come on in. I'll show you the room, okay?" She stepped out and led me down a paved path that wound around the left side of the house. "See that?" she said, pointing, her Bank Hapoalim key chain in her hand. "That's spearmint. Totally natural. You give it a bit of water and it grows on its own. You can pick as much as you want, okay?"

"Thank you."

"There's a fig tree over there that gives fruit the likes of which you'd never find in America. "If it was in season," she added. "Too bad."

"Here it is," she said, standing in front of a brown door set in the middle of a west-facing room. She turned the lock twice and pushed open the door, which led to a chamber that was once an empty space between the pillars that held the second floor aloft. They used to build that way in Tira, too. Bayt ala a'mdan, they'd say of the raised houses that stood perched in the sky on giant concrete legs, and if nothing was built beneath them then they'd leave the space open for parking or kids' games or family events.

"I set everything up for you. Sheets are fresh, towels aplenty, soap and shampoo in the bathroom. I put the Wi-Fi code on the fridge, and inside there's some fresh milk. You must be tired. It's a long flight from America, right? How long is it, twelve hours?"

"Yes."

"Okay, honey, you probably want to get some sleep, so I won't keep blabbering on, but if you want me to make you a cup of tea just say so, okay? And don't be bashful, child, whatever you need just knock on the door. Me and my husband are pretty much home all day. Where do we have to go already? Okay, honey?"

"Very okay," I thanked her, and she left.

It was more than I'd expected for 150 shekels a night.

A double bed with white sheets and blue embroidered trim, just like they have in Tira, and four pillows that the landlord tried to prop up against the headboard as they do in hotels. An old, twenty-one-inch television faced the bed. In the corner of the room there was a kitchenette and a small refrigerator, on the counter a microwave and an electric cooktop with two different-size elements. There were plates and a number of cups on the top shelf of the cabinet and a few basic cooking utensils on the bottom, two small pots, a frying pan, and silverware. There was a small table in the corner of the room with two simple wooden chairs. In the bathroom there was a shower stall with glass doors set nearly flush against the toilet and on the other end of the room a sink with a mirror in a white plastic frame.

I took off my shoes, freeing my feet from two days of bondage. I hadn't wanted to take my shoes off in the hospital, releasing a stench into the room in which my father lay. I lay the trolley suitcase flat next to the bed and as I was trying to work the zipper around the bag I heard a knock at the door.

"Coming," I said and went to open the door.

"I'm sorry for the disturbance," Miriam said, standing with a glass of tea in one hand and a plate of ma'amul cookies in the other. "Don't worry, I won't bother you anymore. I promise. I just figured, why not bring him some tea. It helps after a long trip."

"Thank you so much," I said with a smile and took the tea and cookies, trying to still the tremor that had taken hold of me. "Enjoy," she said and left, leaving me to shut the door and cry into the glass of tea, the color I remembered with the exact right amount of mint leaves floating at just the right level.

What the hell am I doing tearing up over some tea? What does this glass have that makes it seem like it might be the perfect glass of tea, and why is it that when I sip from it I can't help but let the tears flow freely down my face?

3

I woke with a start. The time on my phone said four in the afternoon. I had no missed calls or new messages. My mother doesn't have my number, and no one knows how to get a hold of me. She thinks I'm in Tira. She probably sent one of my brothers to go find me at home, and he could not locate me.

I'd saved my father's cell number and had always made sure it was up-to-date, but I didn't know if his phone was working while he was in the hospital. Nonetheless, I tried calling him with the app, with no success.

I knocked on the door to Miriam's house. "I apologize for the disturbance," I said when she answered, and I asked to use her phone. I was about to explain that I needed to call the hospital and that my phone was American and that I had no way of using it in Israel and that I thought I'd buy a local SIM card but hadn't had the chance, but Miriam just handed me the phone and said, "No disturbance whatsoever, honey. Of course, go ahead."

I called the ICU number that appeared on the hospital website and after a few moments I heard an impatient voice snap: "Intensive care."

"Hello," I said and explained that I was the son of the man in Room 204. "I just wanted to ask —"

"He's not in the ICU anymore," the receptionist said and inquired of the colleague apparently beside her: 'Where did we move the patient that was in two oh four? To the C wing of internal?' He's been moved to internal medicine, Wing C. I'm transferring you now."

"Thank you," I said to the receptionist even though I had not asked to be transferred, wanting only to confirm that he was still alive.

I hung up and thanked Miriam, who said "my pleasure" and added that it was a good sign if someone's moved from the ICU to General Medicine, and may God keep him in good health.

I hadn't eaten a thing since the strips of chicken breast and mashed potatoes that were served on the second leg of the flight from Paris to Tel Aviv, and even Miriam's plate of ma'amul sat untouched on the table in my room. The time was just after eight in the morning on Monday in Illinois, and my phone showed no word from Palestine. She's surely in the car now, I thought, and I won't send her a distracting message while she's driving. She's probably already taken the kids to school and is now on the way to her office on campus. The weather app showed a 20 percent chance of snow, and I hoped that the kids had made it safely to school.

In Kfar Saba and Tira there is never any chance of snow, even though my father told me that one night in the fifties so much snow fell and accumulated overnight that in the morning they weren't able to push open the door and go out into the yard. During our years in Jerusalem it snowed

every now and again and whenever it did it dominated the
news cycle and every year the residents of the city waited
longingly for the arrival of that white wonder. There was a
chance of snow during the week that I got married. It was
the middle of February and the weather forecasters had
their eyes fixed on a storm front moving from Russia to the
Middle East. The rain started as soon as we left Tira. My
father took us to the row of bus stops at the Ra'anana–Kfar
Saba Junction. I sat in the front of the car, my wife in the
back. She was silent for the duration of the ride. The radio
news told of intensifying rain, strong winds that would reach
speeds of eighty kilometers per hour, and snow that would
be falling overnight on Mount Hermon, the high peaks of
the north, and, possibly, Jerusalem.

Palestine had brought just one suitcase with her, and
at the bus stop I helped remove it from my father's trunk.

"You have money?" he asked as he passed me a fifty-
shekel bill even though I had told him that I did. He shook
my wife's hand and said that he was sorry, and that he wished
her all the best in the world.

Palestine stood silently under the bus stop's roof, face
sealed, staring straight ahead in the direction of a point that
didn't exist. She did not cry as is the custom among so many
Arab brides, who are ceremoniously met by the groom and
his coterie at the door of their family houses and accompanied from there to the wedding and from the wedding to a
new house and a new family. The father of the bride holds
the crying bride's hand and leads her to the decorated car,
generally the fanciest car in the extended family's posses-
sion, drafted especially for this mission, and there, in the
back seat, the groom awaits her, in a suit and tie, for the first

time in his life. In the old days, the ceremony was done with horses, and the bride would be lifted onto a horse. But there are no horses left in Tira, so German automobiles have replaced them in the wedding convoy. We took Palestine from her father's house in an undecorated Fiat Punto, with no ululations of joy and no honking to let the public know that a wedding was under way. Her father stowed her suitcase in the trunk, and she got into the back seat alone and said not a word. Instead of a wedding hall, we went to Ra'anana Junction and after a ten-minute wait, the bus showed up and I put her suitcase in the luggage compartment and boarded before her in order to pay for two passengers with the bill my father had put in my hand. I so wanted to sit beside her during that ride, but there were no seats together, so she sat next to a soldier near the front of the bus and I sat a few rows behind her, fixing my gaze on what I was able to see of her head and her long hair, which flowed over her right shoulder. The rain only intensified during the ride, and the radio, which was tuned in to one of the public stations, delivered the forecast at considerable volume and predicted a looming storm and said the chances of snow in Jerusalem are especially high, particularly between midnight and the early morning hours. "If snow falls during those hours," the weatherman said on the radio, "then there's a good chance that it will stick and accumulate. We'll just have to wait and see, because a degree in either direction will prove pivotal."

I was really hoping for snow that night, so we could wake up to a blanket of white. I had been in Jerusalem on days when it had snowed but I presumed that this would be Palestine's first time in a snowy city. We'd wake up together in Jerusalem and the snow would signify a fresh

start, and perhaps we would hug by the window, and if the
snow started to really pile up then we'd head out and make
snowballs, or we'd walk from the college campus on Mount
Scopus to the center of town. I so wanted Palestine to love
Jerusalem, and I was counting on the snow to erase any
longing for the village from her twenty-one-year-old mind.
She did not turn toward me once during the ride. She's so
young, I thought to myself. Granted, I was only two years
older than she was, but still I'd lived in Jerusalem for five
years already, had completed a BA, and was working as
a reporter while pursuing my MA in Hebrew literature. I
knew so little about Palestine back then: I did not know if
she'd gone to college, if she'd ever lived outside the village,
where she'd traveled, what she'd seen, what she loved and
what she hated, if she'd ever taken a bus before, and if she'd
ever been to Jerusalem. And she was so beautiful that when
I first saw her I understood how someone's breath could be
taken away, even though I lowered my eyes when I spoke
a few short sentences to her: "Tfadali." "We get off at the
last stop." "Please let me know if you need anything." I felt
deeply embarrassed by my own excitement, sitting behind a
woman who, on her wedding day, was behaving as though
she were grieving. And how was it that on that morning I'd
still clung to a plan of disengagement, a scheme I'd devised
to disentangle myself from this marriage, which I'd never
considered, never sought, and had been imposed on me on
account of a wretched and lone mistake? For on the morning of the wedding I still despised Palestine with a deathly
vehemence and still planned to do what the sheikh had asked
of me to do — to sign the papers and to take her as my law-
fully wedded wife. But then, upon arrival in Jerusalem,

I planned on sending her on her way and running for it,
even at the price of permanent banishment from that cursed
country. And then I found myself seated a few rows behind
her, incapable of looking away from her back, praying she
would forgive me soon, love me overnight, trusting that the
snow, which may or may not stick, would abolish the sin
and the humiliation.

My phone rang as I lay on the bed in the Aliya tene-
ment. On the screen, in Arabic, the word "Palestine."

"Marhaba, how are you?" I asked, addressing her personally for a change and not using my standard: "How's
everyone?" or "How are the kids?"

"We're fine," she said. "I just called to see how your
father's doing."

"Getting better," I said. "Thank you very much."

"Did you go home?"

"No," I said and wondered if that was why she'd called,
because she was concerned that perhaps I had gone to Tira,
that perhaps I had met someone or spoken with someone
from the village. I didn't go, I said, and I told her about
the room I'd rented near the hospital and that I'd only just
woken up and would soon go back to the hospital, but that
first I had to find something to eat. I felt I was telling her
details that she wasn't interested in, but at times it seems
that these everyday details have the power to calm and cause
forgetfulness.

"Okay," she said. "I just wanted to call and see how
you're doing."

"Thank you," I said and continued. "Palestine . . ."
knowing full well that I was the only person in the world
who called her that.

"What?" she asked. I wanted to tell her that I missed her, that I was sorry, and that I loved her, but all I asked was: "Did it snow?"

"No," she replied. "It didn't."

4

"Come on, tell us, what's up? How you doing? In America, they say. How is it over there? You're so lucky. We wish we all could go. Everything's cheaper there, right? A car is like half the price, no? And how are the kids? How's the wife? Everyone must speak English already no problem. They must be totally American by now, no? But don't you dare let them forget their Arabic, ah, dir balak. Kids are like sponges, they absorb languages like nothing, but they can forget if they don't use it. Actually, how old are your kids? There's three of them, right? Or is it two? Boys? And what do you do over there for work? And how are Muslims treated over there? Either way, it's probably a thousand times better than over here, isn't it? Probably doesn't hurt that you're light skinned, and your wife isn't particularly dark either. Who'd even know where you're from? Trust me, people are jealous of you, what do we have going for us over here, it's hard to know how to raise the kids. Tira, my friend, is not what it once was. It's hell. These days every little punk is carrying a pistol. Where you are it's the same, no, shootings all the time? Any nutjob can buy a gun, no? It's scary, I'm sure it is, but it's nothing like Tira, trust me. And clothes are really cheap over there, aren't they? Shoes that go for two hundred dollars here cost fifty over there. The brand names are much cheaper over there. How much does a Polo shirt cost?

There's homesickness, of course there is, so you come on
over and visit during the summer. What's the big deal? It's
become impossible to live here, just getting worse and worse.
How long you been over there? Two years? During that time
it's become hell here, so that it's terrifying to even think of
taking the kids into Kfar Saba to get them some ice cream.
Netanya, forget it, I haven't been there in six months, maybe
more. They kill Arabs there like it's nothing. Self-defense
and you're free to go. Heeba, our neighbors' daughter, got
pulled out of the college-entrance exam because they were
suspicious of her pencil. I swear to God, a pencil is already
considered a weapon if it's in the hands of an Arab woman,
and she covers her hair, poor thing, a hero, a good student.
Does your wife cover her hair? And what is it that you do
over there? How much do you need to make to live comfort-
ably over there? Here you bust your ass and end up with
nothing. Yesterday they shot Rajeb. You remember Rajeb?
He was like a grade behind you. Come on, Rajeb, the man,
Fathi's brother. Over nothing, five caps in the legs, they
say he's going to need a new knee, an implant made out
of metal. And for what? A father of four. Some say it had
something to do with a woman. Others say it was a clash
over parking. These days there's no need for reasons, no
matter what you say they come out shooting, spraying you
with bullets. There's a new generation coming up, and God
help us you can't say a word to these kids. Where's the old
Tira gone, and when's it coming back? These days you feel
like you're rolling the dice every time you go and pick your
kids up from school. You wait around all day till you know
they've been scooped up and are safe at home. And what
about teachers, you think they don't get shot? In school,

with no shame at all. There's nowhere to run to. The family here with you? Where are they, let's have a look. You have pictures of the kids? Too bad, how old are they? Wow, hard to believe, feels as though it all happened just yesterday. Trust me, you have to get to know the extended family, bring them for a visit to Tira. You have to. You know what they say: someone who's not good to his parents isn't good to anyone. No, I didn't mean, of course it was difficult, but halas, enough, it's a new generation now. Everything's different. Look at your father. If he makes it through this year who's to say he'll make it through the next one. They should get to know their cousins, their family. What's a man worth without his family? He'll always be a stranger. With God's help your father will stay on the mend. These days medicine does miracles. With God's help. What's the dollar rate these days? Four, maybe a little less, something like three eighty-five? How much does a hamburger cost over there? Here McDonald's sells a meal at forty-five shekels. How much does it cost you over there? And your mother, you know, she's not that young anymore, and it hurts, for sure, it hurts to leave the parents like that. Especially, if, heaven forbid, your father … may he live a long life. You know, what will she have in her life aside from her children? And besides it's been a long time, people forget, people forgive, and you are already a man and your wife's a woman and your kids are big, no one will say a word to you."

Two of my cousins sat on benches facing the entrance to the internal medicine department, even though I'd been careful to arrive at the hospital after seven in the evening, at which time visiting hours were over to all but the immediate family. They just sat there, having already seen their uncle. "Alhamdulillah, he looks a lot better. With God's help he'll be home soon," they said to one another.

"They're just waiting for Dad to die," my youngest brother said once the cousins were gone. My older brother had left without a word as soon as he saw me coming.

"They haven't remotely waited for him to die," the brother two years younger than me said. "I wish they would have waited for his death before starting the war."

This was my first time meeting my brothers' wives. Walid, my older brother, majored in economics at Ben-Gurion University and has a good job at a bank. He got married three years after me. His wife's from Tira, an educational adviser at the middle school, and they have two boys. The older one is in sixth grade and the younger one is in first. The brother who is two years younger than me, Tarek, is an accountant who ten years ago married an elementary school teacher from Tira, and they have a son in third grade and another on the way. His wife is in her eighth month of pregnancy. The two met as undergrads at Tel Aviv University. My youngest brother, Hamouda, came accompanied by his wife, also a teacher with a full-time position and a job as a substitute teacher at the elementary school in Tira.

My younger brothers and their wives wanted me to meet their kids. I must come back to Tira they said, and if not then they'll bring the kids to the hospital tomorrow. My brothers swear that the kids have heard only good things about me from their parents and grandparents, stories about how well behaved I was and what a sharp student I was. "He's smart as his uncle," the educational adviser said, quoting my father, who liked to compare me to her firstborn, because he, too, is the top student in his class and is also enrolled in the program for gifted children. There's no need to apologize they said when I told them how much I wish I'd been at their weddings. They have photo albums and videotapes of the events and will be happy to show them to me.

We have neither albums nor video footage of our wedding and have even managed to forget the true date of our anniversary, having taken a new date, which is properly in sync with the birth of our daughter.

I last saw my three brothers as I left the family house and drove off with my father to Palestine's home. My older brother hugged me hard back then, and the little one cried because he did not understand the sadness that had permeated the house and why all of this was happening. They were not witnesses to the wedding. Only the two cousins, those I met at the hospital, accompanied me and my father, a convoy of three cars, in front of and behind the used Fiat Punto my father had only recently bought. The ceremony was less than five minutes long. The father of the bride did not shake my hand; he took my father's instead. The sheikh placed a cloth kerchief over the clasped hands of the two fathers, asked several terse questions, murmured a few words of prayer, and then had me sign some papers and turned toward an interior room, where I assumed he was signing Palestine to the same contract.

❋   ❋   ❋

A biting Jerusalem cold greeted us as we got off at the Central Bus Station. Palestine had no coat, and I so wanted to offer her mine, but the tongue, the cursed tongue, spoke not a word. We took a taxi to the Mount Scopus dorms. Palestine sat in back and I sat beside the driver. I had a single room, one of the privileges offered to students pursuing advanced degrees. I had taken the room's two single beds, which in America they call twin size, and pushed them together and up against the north wall of the room, far from the window. When Palestine walked into the room I separated the beds and returned them to their original spots, one pressed against the south wall and the other against the north wall. "Are you hungry?" I asked Palestine, and I handed her a towel for her wet hair. She shook her head. "Can you leave me alone" was the first sentence she spoke to me.

~~On the morning after the wedding, Jerusalem was blanketed in white.~~

I was then not yet twenty-two and Palestine was not yet twenty-one; eight months later our daughter was born, on the day that yet another war broke out. I remember that I smoked my first cigarette that day, in a small, square garden trapped between concrete walls just outside the obstetrics department of the Hadassah Medical Center. That morning we'd taken a taxi to the hospital for a routine prenatal checkup. That morning my wife felt nothing unusual and no contractions. They gave her an ultrasound in the maternity ward and connected her to a fetal heart rate monitor. Then they put these straps around her with electrodes that were connected to a monitor and a thin needle that drew lines on a moving sheet of paper. The midwife said Palestine's cervix was dilated and that the birth was imminent. She asked that we not leave the hospital grounds and suggested that we do some labor-hastening exercises, such as going up and down the stairs.

The contractions started soon afterward. When we got back to the maternity ward the nurse examined Palestine again and moved her into a delivery room in order to properly prepare for the birth. Palestine asked for an epidural and the nurse recommended that being young, strong, and healthy she try a natural birth. "There's nothing about this birth that's natural," my wife said in Arabic, so that the midwife wouldn't understand and I would.

"Out," she said to me as the contractions intensified. The television in the waiting room broadcast silent images of destruction—a building between crosshairs and then a spiral of smoke, at first black and then white.

I so wanted to be a supportive husband in the delivery room, like in the movies. I'd hoped that my wife would let me hold her hand while she pushed and breathed and sweated, that moments before the sound of crying would be heard a sublime smile would settle across her face, the smile only a mother can produce, and she'd raise her eyes to meet mine in a look that says thank you, that says I love you, I forgive you.

Through the waiting room's glass window, I saw an ultra-Orthodox man smoking and speaking on a cell phone. I waited for him to finish his conversation and then I went outside.

"Can I have a cigarette, please?" I asked.

"Your first?" the religious man asked, smiling at me and propping a cigarette out of his red Marlboro box.

"Yes," I said, and I didn't know if he meant birth or cigarette. I tried smothering the cough of that inhalation as the religious man said that everything would be okay, God willing.

5

"I'm scared," my father said once we were left alone and the nurses had shut off the overhead lights in the room.

"Of what?" I asked, surprised. I had never heard my father pair those two words together and was curious to hear what would follow.

"Scared of what?" I asked again.

"I'm scared," he said slowly. "Scared to death." His pale, unsmiling face didn't flinch.

I was more prepared for my father's death than for his fear. Now I know what sort of expression settles on the face of a man who fears death; now I know that all those interviewees who said they were not afraid were lying. They lied when they said that they'd fulfilled all of their desires, raised children, cradled grandchildren, and what else is there to aspire to? They were just trying to soothe themselves: if they didn't fear death, it wouldn't come for them, as though death were a dog with the ability to sense fear and attack.

"You've got nothing to be afraid of," I stammered, mostly in order to break the silence in the room. But my father did not want to be comforted. "I'm scared": it was just him stating a fact, telling me how it was, a glimpse at the truth, telling me that you, too, will be filled with fear. You will not be concerned or worried but truly afraid.

"But look, Dad," I tried to say, "they moved you from the ICU to General Medicine. That's good news."

"This is where they put those who can't get better."

I protested, telling him this is not a hospice. There are patients of all different ages here.

"Can you bring me some water, please?" asked my father, who was still not allowed to get out of bed.

"Dad," I called to him just as I had silently done over the past fourteen years.

"What, my son?" he answered.

I wanted to tell my father what I figured fathers want to hear about their sons, a story that I had prepared in advance, practiced, and repeated to myself. I told him that I owned a publishing house now that made pretty good money. We publish people's memoirs and biographies and are hired by sons and daughters who buy our services as a present for their elderly parents, especially those who have incredible life stories that the children would like to see published in book form. I told my father that I send my employees to interview the clients and that this work takes up all of my time in America, that up until the moment the kids come back from school I am transcribing and editing people's memoirs and that my wife has a doctorate in psychology and that she accepted a position from a large American university and that the kids go to the best schools and are very happy and have made lots of friends and learned the language and are now fully fluent in three languages: Hebrew, Arabic, and English. Only we missed all of you the whole time over there, but you know, we can still change that, maybe. What do you say, Dad? Can I record you and then write your story? And if you don't like it then I'll toss it out, and no one will ever know.

You didn't learn a thing from the woe that your writing has wrought?

I learned a lot of things, Dad. Ever since that cursed story I only write the truth. Nothing fabricated, I promise.

And back then it wasn't the truth that you wrote?

So what do you say, Dad? I'll record a bit until you get tired. Just tell me, and I'll stop.

What do you want to record?

"I always start with the same question," I told my father, peeling the cellophane wrapper from a new cassette. I inserted it and pressed Record.

"What's your first memory?" I asked my father, setting the tape recorder on the food tray so that the microphone would be as close as possible to his mouth.

"I didn't bring you here from America to talk about my first memory," my father said. "Maybe it would be better to start with the last memory I have of you."

I said nothing, and my father suddenly blurted out: "Why'd you come?" And I didn't know if he meant why did I come to see him now or why did I come then, to Tira, on the day of the wedding.

Why'd you come?

On that day, too, he had placidly asked me the same question, disappointed that I'd showed up after he'd firmly told me not to show myself again in Tira or in the vicinity of the village. He was so opposed to the marriage with Palestine that he was willing to be the target of degradation, threats, gossip, and defamation, in both the cafés that he frequented and the mosques that he boycotted. "You think you're doing something noble?" he spat at me when I arrived at the home, determined to marry her as some of the family's representatives had demanded, claiming that this was a reasonable compromise according to the accepted norms. Once I showed up, in violation of my father's dictates, there was no longer the option of regret. I had broken something and I would fix it. That is what I thought then and that is what I still think today.

"I came to be with you, Dad," I told him. "I came to be with you."

"Do you have pictures of the kids?" he asked.

"Yes. I do, but don't tell anyone that I have, okay? I didn't even show them to Mom."

"Your secret will go with me to my grave," he said and smiled for the first time that evening. I showed my father a series of pictures that I had curated on my phone, with the understanding that I might have to display them. I left only those that told a warm family story. He could flip through them himself, look at my smiling wife and kids. Granted, there were no photos of me and Palestine together with the kids, but that's because someone had to take the photographs. My father examined the photos for many long moments and then asked what the little one's name was and why his hair was curly, and he said it's clear that he's the little rascal. "Well, I don't see all that well, and I don't even remember what your wife looks like anymore. And the girl, she's huge. Is she always this serious or does she smile sometimes? How old is she? Thirteen? She looks older."

I told my father that my daughter was always the tallest kid in the class, that in America they measure height in feet and inches and that she's six foot two, tall like her mother, around one meter, eighty-five. The youngest one is also the tallest in his kindergarten, and only the middle one is average height for his age.

"They already look American," my father said. "I bet no over there knows where they're from."

"Yes," I replied. "There it's different."

"When was the girl born?" my father said, asking the question that I had been rehearsing the answer to for all these years.

"She was born in December," I said. "Just last month she had her thirteenth birthday."

The eleventh of December, ten months after the wedding. That's what Palestine and I — my wife and I — decided would be the birth date of our daughter, our firstborn, if we were asked to provide answers.

6

Dad.

What?

Should we record, Dad?

You say "dad" a lot.

It's weird for me to address you aloud.

You've addressed me in silence?

Every day.

Do I respond?

Sometimes, yes.

I always respond.

I'm recording, okay?

Your tape recorder is on. You're already recording.

Okay. When you get tired, let me know, okay, Dad?

I slept all day, maybe two days straight, strange that I'm passing the last days I have in sleep.

Don't say that.

Actually, what could be better than sleep.

Right, let's start. So, what's your first memory, Dad?

Not being able to remember.

Do you want me to stop?

No. My first memory is of not being able to remember. I wake up, not from sleep but from daydreaming, and I know that something awful has happened, but I can't remember what, and your grandmother tells me: 'Asem Allah alik, ya habibi, asem Allah alik.' And she asks, 'What's the matter, ya habibi. What's bothering you?' And I can't tell of the terrible thing I've forgotten, and I tell my mother that I can't remember and am filled with pain.

How old were you?

Don't know. Maybe four or five. To this day I don't really know how old I am. It's always been one year this way or that. Bring me some more water.

Sure. Sip it slowly Are you tired, Dad?

I don't know. I want a cigarette. Do you have one?

No.

Are you still lying?

What do you mean a cigarette? After a heart attack? Come on, Dad.

What will they do to me if I smoke in the room? What could they possibly do to me? It's too late for me anyway.

Don't say that.

You're right. I won't say it, and it isn't true, either. It isn't the heart that nearly killed me.

Dad!

I'm tired.

Okay, don't worry. I'll stop.

Keep recording. Maybe I'll listen and you'll tell me.

What? A bedtime story?

Make it a story with a happy end, okay?

What do you want me to tell you, Dad?

What is permitted and what is forbidden to tell a sick father.

May I say that I am a bit jealous of you, would like to be in your place, in your sickbed? May I beg my father to stay alive, because without him I'll be more afraid and will have a harder time going to sleep? May I tell him that I need him, because despite the distance I still console myself with the fact that I can always run back to him if the situation worsens? May I tell him that I'm almost forty and that all I want is to sit in his lap in the driver's seat, holding the wheel as we drive along the paths of the orchards that no longer exist? What can I tell him? That ever since I left I dream only of returning, that I need his approval, that I need him to promise me that everything will be okay if I go back to Tira, that it's safe, like it once was—or like I want to remember it having been? Is it permissible to tell a sick father that I'm still scared at nights and that I'll always wander between the house and the elementary school, afraid of getting lost?

That I miss the red loamy soil around the back of the house, especially in the spring, when it's still moist. That I'm saddened for my children who have never dug into the sand, that the claylike earth has never slid beneath their fingernails as they look for earthworms. That they don't know that the gecko doesn't care if you cut off her tail and that she grows a new one to replace the old. Geckos are evil and may be killed, because they told on the Prophet Muhammad and revealed his hiding spot to the infidels who pursued him. And that snakes shed their skins in the spring, and you can play with the skin once it dries out a bit in the sun and where there are skins there are also snakes so you have to be careful.

I miss the chameleons. I'd watch them change colors on the tree and the concrete wall that separated our house from the neighbors' house. I want to be stung again by the honeybees, which we tried to play with, putting some juice in a plastic bag and looking for bees among the sabras flowers.

When we managed to catch one in the bag we would wait for it to turn the sugary juice into honey, but that never happened, and at times we were stung. I didn't know if the bee realized that it would die then or if it was always surprised, not having intended on suicide. If stung, we'd have to pull out the stinger and rub the infected skin with onion, though some kids contended that the proper cure was rubbing a tomato on the surface of the bite. And wasps must be watched out for, because a wasp sting in a very sensitive area could kill you. If by chance you encountered a wasp you had to stand still and not move until it flew off. And you have to be mindful of leaves when picking figs because they can cause a rash, and if you pick the fruit before it's ripe, you need to watch out for the thick white tree sap. The fig tree is blessed because it covered the nakedness of the son of God. And the pumpkin, too, is blessed because God sent it to cover the prophet Jonah when he was spit out naked onto the shore from the belly of the whale. I always wanted to ask the adults how it was that the fig leaves did not itch our forefather Adam and how it was that pumpkin flowers suddenly grew in the sandy soil of the shore, which everyone knows is too salty to produce plants. But I did not ask because I knew that every tree and every sort of soil would obey a direct order from God.

And the loquat mustn't be picked when it's still green, even though it's good when it's unripe, so long as it's dipped in a bit of salt, which sticks to the skin, revealing a pleasant sour taste that burns the lips and the palate. The green almonds are also good to eat with salt, when the inner nut is still white and soft. And you have to watch out for the thorns when picking lemons and be sure to tear the right size branch off the lemon tree and strip the green layer off the wood, leaving it bare and white, and I'd know it was right if I heard the precise whistling sound I was looking for when I whipped the naked branch through the air. And then I had to stand straight, trying not to move, because if I moved and the branch did not strike my body at the right angle I'd have to get another stroke, even if the inaccurate one already hurt. So it was best to stand still and not move, and there was no sense in clenching your muscles, even though they couldn't be relaxed even if you really wanted to, and the whistling branch burnt, and it took time for the pain to spread, and you felt a sort of flame across the skin, and a desire to rub it with your hand, but you couldn't, and you had to wait for all of the blows to land on the body, and at first the skin was covered with red stripes, which turned purple the following day and green the day after that and then dark, and within seven days you could wear shorts again, but you didn't have to.

Two months later, seated at the dorm room desk, I look at a new file, which I'd like to save as "Dad edited":

~~My first memory is of not being able to remember. I wake up, not from sleep but from gazing, and I know that something awful has happened, but I can't remember what, and your grandmother she tells me, "Asem Allah alik, ya habibi, asem Allah alik." And she asks, "What's the matter, ya habibi? What's bothering you?" And I can't tell of the terrible thing I've forgotten, and I tell my mother that I can't remember and am filled with pain.~~

"My first memory is of a picture of your grandmother, sitting beneath two giant eucalyptus trees that I used to love to climb when she wasn't looking. In my memory, she's sitting along with a few of the women from the neighborhood and family, and they're singing happy songs and cooking sweet awameh balls in big pots over orange flames from the wood of a lemon tree."

D

1

During the nights of fitful sleep, I realized that I'd never managed to get over the jetlag, never managed to bridge the time difference between Jerusalem and Illinois. During those rare nights that my wife requested my presence in the family home, on the ground-floor couch, which we bought together from a secondhand site, it seemed to me that my sleep was seamless and serene, even though I generally spent the whole night awake hoping that Palestine might want to talk or might hug me in silence and stroke my hair until I fell asleep.

I'm the only one who calls my wife Palestine. Her parents gave her that name — Falasteen, in Arabic — because she was born on the thirtieth of March, five years after Land Day. In those days people still had faith in the PLO, in the Fedayeed, in the national struggle. Once she told me that she doesn't remember anyone ever calling her by that name, that at home she was called Fofo, and in class Faula. Even the teachers preferred calling her Faula, like the flower, fearing the open eyes of the Ministry of Education supervisors and the prohibition against speaking of Palestine in the national school system.

Once we were married she changed her name officially
to Faula, and at times, when her name was called at a hospital or a government institution, they dropped the single
dot that differentiated the F and P sound and pronounced it
Paula, like Ben-Gurion's wife. She changed her family name
to Hadad, and when our daughter was born I switched my
family name, too, on my identity card.

I had known nothing of Palestine's existence. She was a
character in a short story, a very short story I had written. I
had imagined the contours of her face and drew her features
in my mind's eye: the length of her neck; the shape of her
black eyes; the curve of her eyelashes, which were draped
in mascara; her eyebrows darkened with kohl. I described
her dimples, which winked when she spoke and kissed, and
her long hair, which fell across her shoulders. I imagined
her hips and the perfect line they drew toward her pelvis. I
described her proud breasts and nipples, which stood erect
without fear. It was a wretched story that I wrote quickly
before one of our Thursday night get-togethers at the bar.
I was the only Arab reporter at that paper, the only one in
the group, and anything I wrote was welcomed with compli-
ments that I didn't fully believe, unsure to what extent they
were the truth or affirmative action. Those were different
days, the days between Rabin's murder and the Al-Aqsa
Intifada. Despite the election-night loss to the Right, shortly
after Rabin's assassination there had been a sense that this
was a temporary farce that would soon be corrected.
    I wrote "Palestine" after learning in one of my litera-
ture classes about a writer who described his homeland as

a woman and colonialism as masculine. I did not put much
weight in what I had written; it was nothing more than a
page from the desk of an amateur scribe, brought, out of a
sense of duty, to a social evening. The story, written in less
than an hour in my dorm room, was narrated in first person
and about a high school student from Tira who on Independence Day sleeps with a girl whose name is Palestine. It was
a wretched little piece, less than a thousand words long, full
of clichés and descriptions of sex that I thought, because
written by a conservative Arab, would be considered au-
dacious by my friends. I wrote about how the love-struck
student uses the compulsory holiday of Independence Day,
which is forced upon him annually, in order to meet the
object of his desire on the roof of the local high school in
Tira, which they both attend, and there, under the flag that
is flown once a year, the symbol of loyal citizenship, they first
sleep together, losing their virginity, and, filled with shame
and humiliation, they are filled with mournful regret. The
story garnered praise from the other members of the group.
"You have to publish this," the paper's TV critic, who every
now and again wrote a poem no one understood, said. "You
just have to," he added and mentioned an acquaintance who
could submit the story to the editors of the student magazine
at Hebrew U.

I handed him the page, torn out of my notebook.

Two months later the journal printed my story. I remember how filled with joy I was at the sight of my name
on the page, at the tender age of twenty-two, an Arab who
writes in Hebrew. It was the real thing: not some article
in the weekly fish wrap, but literature, the sort that only a
chosen few are able to produce. This was a green light for

dreams I had that up until then had not been put into motion. I was no longer bothered by the suspicions that I was being published or praised by my friends simply because they expected less of me, and that, perhaps, the simple fact of my being able to string together a few sentences in their language was perceived as a feat worthy of wonder. I was not bothered by the fact that I'd written a short story on the basis of a sentence I'd heard about the homeland as a woman. And I had completely forgotten that when I'd put my pen down I'd thought that it was shallow and predictable. I was simply happy, and I already dared to believe that I was to be counted among literary writers. Aside from my colleagues at the paper, my friends from the Thursday night writing crew, I didn't know if there was anyone else who had read "Palestine."

Nonetheless, after my initial excitement, I was assaulted by angst and self-loathing. I imagined my teachers in the literature department making fun of me behind my back. I imagined the head of the department sitting in his office chuckling with the rest of the faculty about the Arab student who wants to be Anton Shammas, and in the end just winds up fucking the homeland in broken Hebrew beneath the blue-and-white flag.

Then, after several weeks of not hearing a word from anyone about the story, I forgot about it entirely and my angst and sorrow died down, too. It was more than a year later that my father called me.

"Did you write a story about Palestine?" he asked.

It took me some time to comprehend the question and to remember and I answered with a prideful yes but was soon overcome with concern. After all, it was not for nothing that I didn't tell my parents about the story or show them copies of the issue during my monthly visits to Tira. I had written about the alcohol consumed by both characters as they looked out at the landscape of their youth from the school rooftop, a landscape that was once a quilt of strawberry fields and fig trees now crowded with a rash of metal shops and garages, their signs advertising devoted service and reduced prices for Jewish customers in mistake-ridden Hebrew. The story I wrote was not for the residents of Tira, not in their language, not on their behalf, not in their names. I never once considered that it would reach Arab hands. And now, somehow, it had made its way into my father's hands.

"It's just a story." I tried to soothe my father, to convey that I was still the same good kid that he had sent to Jerusalem, capable of imagining and writing but certainly not of the acts described in the story.

"A story it is," my father said, and I could sense the concern in his voice, though he kept his cool. "You never wrote this story, though," he went on. "Do you understand? You have nothing to do with this story, if anyone asks. And you watch out for yourself over there. For now, it's best that you sleep over at the house of a friend that you trust, until I say otherwise. You understand?"

"I don't understand."

"And no matter what, don't go anywhere near Tira."

2

Palestine had a suitcase, old but well crafted, a top-of-the-line brand, and she brought it with her when she left Tira. Sometimes I wondered if she had ever been out of the country before we were married, maybe on a honeymoon somewhere in Europe or maybe in America before we flew over there together for the first time.

She was the only one in the family who had a passport, but it was expired. She brought that, too, with her from Tira when we left, but she forgot her identity card and later we had to have a new one issued. She told the clerk at the Ministry of Interior in Jerusalem that she'd lost her old identity card and that she wanted to have a new one made and for her name to be changed, both first and last. When we started planning our trip to Illinois, she insisted that her old suitcase was perfectly fine, and there was no reason to get a new one. The kids and I had never been out of the country, and the few trips we'd taken down to Eilat or the Dead Sea or Tiberias, we'd done with gym bags of different sizes.

When you leave the country, though, you need a suitcase. So we bought four new pieces of luggage, two large cases — for me and my daughter — and two small ones for the boys.

The suitcase sizes were determined by volume of memories, which was determined by age: the little ones grow fast and gain at least a size each year, so other than some summer clothes, which we knew they would need for the first few weeks, we decided to buy everything else there, when we got to America. We were told clothes are cheap there and anyway we knew they'd need a whole new wardrobe, suitable clothing for the long, hard winters they had yet to experience.

"You can only take two toys," I told my son, who was then three. And in order to verify that he understood I repeated myself, this time in Hebrew: "Only two, cutie," I said and promised him I would buy him whatever he needed when we got to America. "There are giant toy stores there," I said, and I accompanied the statement with hand gestures, working to convince him or perhaps myself—so we'd know we were going somewhere deserving and better. My little son cried, not understanding why he had to abandon his old toys and why we were leaving. His older brother, who shared a room with him, didn't say a word as he packed his little suitcase. "Take only the things that you really, really love," I told him, and he nodded and said that he didn't need any toys and that there was room in his suitcase for his brother to bring two more.

My daughter asked that she be left alone, and she locked her bedroom door. She didn't need help from anyone she said and would be fine on her own. Everything happened so fast that summer. It had been a year since my wife had received the offer and, left with no other choice, I had consented to go. Then during the final weeks before departure, still very much unready, we decided to move the departure date up by two months. I could not wait until mid-August to leave Jerusalem.

That summer fires ringed the city. Smoke spiraled up from the Jerusalem Forest every day and curtained off the sky. Three teenage settlers were kidnapped. The percussion of helicopter propellers and the wails of ambulances, fire trucks, and police cars reverberated throughout the city. Somehow, it was the fires that bothered me the most. I was scared that the flames would grab hold of the buildings in the neighborhood and burn them down and there would be nowhere to run to and no way to defend ourselves from the advancing heat. I've never had such a fear of fire as during those final days in Jerusalem. The news reports said it was Arabs who had started them. Everyone knew it was Arabs, even though in most cases it turned out that the fires were sparked by hikers or kids in summer camps of one sort or another. But that never changed a thing and that summer especially it was clear that the Arabs were guilty.

Every day, whenever the secretary in the newsroom saw me, she started swishing spit around her mouth and then hurled it into the garbage. The reporters sent in their copy and I kept their barbed anti-Arab prose intact, didn't ask questions, didn't ask for facts to be checked. The education reporter filed stories from the abducted teens' schools; the police beat reporter wrote of the danger of the Arab residents of the city; and the city hall reporter told of the sanctions planned against the vendors and residents of those neighborhoods. The pictures of the three boys were the only ones we ran on the pages of the two editions that I edited, from their abduction to their discovery. And once they were found, lifeless, the fires only intensified, the smoke thickening over the Kiryat HaYovel neighborhood. That summer is when I first realized that I wanted to leave even more than Palestine. Even though I knew that there, once we arrived, she would surely set new rules to our joined lives. Sometimes I hoped that there, aided by distance and isolation, we'd start over again, as though we'd just met for the first time. Maybe I'd send her flowers or love letters and with time would invite her out to a movie or to dinner.

On the day of the funerals for the three boys, Palestine stayed home from work with the kids, who, out of a fear of Jewish vengeance, were not permitted to leave the house. I had no choice but to go to the newsroom and edit the articles about the funerals, the interviews with the bereaved families, the neighbors, the friends from school and the rabbis, and the comforting feeling of unity that settled over the nation in its mourning. A deep, honest, and pure mourning, to which strangers are not admitted and the essence of which they will never know.

On Wednesday morning, the day after the funerals and the subsequent stalking of Arab workers on the streets of Jerusalem, there was a news report of a suspected kidnapping of an Arab child in one of the city's southern neighborhoods. My wife said that maybe we should move up our flights. After all, the academic year was finished, all the tests had been given, and the final grades could always be uploaded into the computer system from the United States. Before heading off to work that day I bought bread and eggs at the local grocery store, and Palestine stayed home and promised

to lock the door and bolt the shutters. I had that week's issue
of the paper and then two more issues to put to bed and my
tenure as editor was over. I'd already given advance notice.
The radio news in the car reported that a charred body had
been found in the Jerusalem Forest, and even though on
that day there was no smoke and the sky was clearer than
it had been all summer, the charred scent rising up in my
nostrils was redolent of hair and skin, muscles and bones,
intestines and a heart.

I felt repulsed by that hideous glimmer of hope. The
hope that this human sacrifice would redeem the souls of my
children. The secretary greeted me as always with an audible
spit into the trash can, and the janitor from East Jerusalem
who cleans up after her did not show up to work on that
day. Here, now they've burnt a live child, and maybe that
will slake their thirst for revenge and put things back on
the track of routine brutality, the rules of which we already
know. I need to hold on for just two more issues after this
week and then we'll have two weeks to pack, get organized,
and get out of here.

The police reporter filed a news piece stating that the
Arab boy had been killed by members of his own family.

According to the information he submitted, the Arab
boy was a homosexual who had been abused in the past by
his family members, who had tried in the past to abduct him
on several occasions. The police started an investigation,
looking for the family members who had burnt the child
while still alive.

During those torrid days it was not possible to ask
questions or poke holes in the veracity of the reports. This

version of events was being written up by all of the police reporters, and it was the version the unified public believed in. The publisher, in a rather unusual move, showed up in the newsroom to make sure that I ran the piece about the murder actually being the result of an honor killing. In truth, he knew I would run it; he just wanted to make sure that I felt the scorn he had for me. I read through the piece, which was given top real estate on the front page, and I chose a picture that had been distributed by the police spokespeople, in which a Palestinian youth, maybe twelve years old, was depicted in a selfie that had served as a profile picture for Facebook or some other site, his hair shaved on the sides, his face delicate and pretty. That was the story that was sent to print on the front page of the Jerusalem weekly paper on Thursday night and distributed to stores on Friday morning.

With only three issues of the paper left to produce, I worked with the office door shut. No one came in, not even the janitor, who used to empty the trash and share a cigarette with me. Maybe he was afraid and maybe he was tired of the routine. I was afraid and I was tired of it. I edited the issue: the teens' funerals, the pictures of their smiling faces in school yards and on field trips, and a gay Arab boy who must have known how to dance the debka, or not and maybe would have joined the circles of dancers and maybe would have stood off to the side, watching and learning. I don't know how to dance. How is it possible that I never learned to do the debka? How is it that all of the boys, already in middle school, danced at the weddings and knew how to link arms and stamp feet and I never managed to learn the rhythm of the circle, which leg to raise when, how to memorize the moves, when to dip with the knees. How is it that I never managed to dance with my chest puffed out, my movements sure? My cousins would ask me how I intended to dance the traditional dance with the bride, and they laughed that I wouldn't know what to do and they didn't imagine that I wouldn't have a wedding or a party or a song or a circle for the debka. My kids don't know how to dance, and they don't even know that they don't know. They don't know any wedding songs or how threatening they can sometimes sound. Wedding singers are always men and they are capable of saying some bold things about women. The women are always sashaying to the well to draw water. They are beautiful and noble, and the pitchers sit steady atop their heads. And the men are always strong hunters. The women are gazelles; the men are lions. Palestine was surely a gazelle and her husband surely knew how to dance and had no fear of the wedding songs and their bold verses of praise for women.

I left the office only when I knew there was no secretary waiting outside the door, no publisher, no advertising salespeople. And rather than go home I drove to the Malha Mall, my head down, avoiding eye contact with passersby, knowing that their gazes were clouded with hatred and fear. I had no desire to be antagonized by their identity-probing stares, as they tried to figure out whether or not I was one of them or the enemy. All I wanted was to buy four pieces of luggage, two big, two small.

On the morning that a yellow flame flared from the child in the Jerusalem Forest, Palestine informed me of the flight change. "We'll leave tomorrow," she said. "There are seats available because people are canceling flights, and we'll have to pay a two-hundred-dollar fine."

Tomorrow? And what will we do with the apartment? The car? I need the money, even though it isn't worth all that much. But I'll just have to leave it at a used car lot. I have no choice. We won't have time to store the furniture in the storage unit that I intended to rent for three years, for chances are we won't be back. Palestine will surely find a way to stay in America, and she'll allow me to stay with her and not push me away from the children. She wouldn't do that to me.

The kids will be fine.

Kids grow accustomed to any situation.

And the furniture?

Don't know.

And the car?

And the apartment?

We'll leave it all and run. We'll tell the owner of the apartment that we moved up our trip. We'll leave him everything, and he'll do what he pleases. If he's nice, he'll reimburse us in some way and maybe the new tenants will want some of the stuff.

We'll shut off our electricity.

We'll empty the fridge.

One suitcase per person, it'll suffice.

We'll disconnect the gas.

The phone.

The main waterline.

We'll call the apartment owner in the morning and discuss the furniture with him, maybe he'll keep it for us?

And the toys.
Two toys for each of them will do.

The next morning, I did not go into the newsroom, and no one called to see how I was doing.

3

Ever since arriving here I shave only once a week, on Friday mornings, as opposed to every other day the way I used to do in Jerusalem. My father used to shave every morning using a green shaving gel that he rubbed into his left and right cheek. Every morning he'd heat water for coffee in a tin pot and before the water came to a boil he'd splash a bit into a plastic cup into which he'd dip his wood-handled shaving brush. When the brush bristles were wet and softened he would rub them across his short scruff in a precise circular motion, and the green cream would turn into a white foam. He would stiffen his lips and draw the brush up under his nose and then relax his lips so that the foam wouldn't go into his mouth.

Dad's razors were thin, rectangular, double-edged, and he would peel off the white wrapper every morning and place the blade in a stick with a jagged wheel at the bottom; a clockwise turning of the wheel would open the doors of the razor head and once the blade had been stably inserted, the wheel was turned in the opposite direction and the doors held the razor in place, so that the double-edged razor stuck out just the right amount on either side.

He'd place his left forefinger above his cheekbone, stretching the skin upward, knowing exactly where he'd place the blade so that his sideburns would be at just the right height, and then he'd drag the blade, in long and steady strokes, toward his chin. Then he'd turn the razor head around and pull in the other direction. After going both ways, on either side of his face, he'd shake the razor in the cup of warm water and do it again. Straight, precise lines, which do not require more than one pass on the already revealed skin, free of soap and stubble, which with the years went from black to white.

I would watch him and learn, and he would smile at me from the sink mirror, which was fixed on the back of the living room wall. Sometimes he would wink at me in the mirror and momentarily break the spell of the blade's motion. He would wash his face with two cupped hands, holding an impressive amount of water, like those cowboys in the movies who would wash off outside the ranch, always knowing how to curve and seal their heavy hands in just the right way, filling them with water from a barrel. Using the towel that hung from his shoulder and never fell even when he bent over, my father would dry his face and look in the mirror, and then wipe his ears and neck, making sure that no wayward shaving cream had gotten stuck there, and none ever did.

When I stand before the mirror in my dorm on Friday morning, with a razor that can't cut the skin and a foam that is produced with the pressing of a button and requires no lathering, my heart aches that my boys are not watching me. Maybe I'll bring them here one day, and I'll shave with the door open, so that they can peek, because there are no longer mirrors and sinks in open spaces, made for guests to be able to wash their hands after meals without entering the hosts' bathrooms. Up until then I'll have to work on my hesitant motions, practicing long strokes with the blade, raising my head, pulling my skin taut, being decisive, moving the razor in sharp straight lines, even if it hurts a bit.

I want to take the kids for a long drive in the car. Maybe Palestine will come, too. It will start getting warmer soon, and I'll take a look at the map and go for a drive with the kids, like my family used to do when we were young. Mom and Dad in the front seat and us kids in the back — packed in and fighting over who will sit by the window and who will be squished in the middle — asking Dad to go fast and Mom begging him to slow down. And he would say this car couldn't go fast even if I wanted it to, and the windows would be open, a strong, pleasant wind blowing in our faces.

I will have to take a drive with the kids. Maybe we'll find za'atar growing in Illinois, and we'll forage and fill up sacks. During our excursions with Dad, up into the hills where the herb grows, we'd always be on the lookout for the nature "insbektors," as the adults pronounced it, though I never once saw them. "The insbektors will confiscate the za'atar if they catch us," the adults would warn. "Which is why we need to be careful, because sometimes they fine and even arrest Arabs, depending on the amount of za'atar they are able to seize." I loved the way the za'atar grew between the rocks, but I was very scared that the insbektors would seize my haul. I was scared and my father always said I shouldn't be scared, that the za'atar was ours and that no insbektor could tell us what was ours and what was not, what we could eat and what we could not. The za'atar was here before them and it would be here after them, and the za'atar would stop growing if it saw it was no longer wanted. The za'atar was ours; it always was. And it had to be picked in season and prepared right away, dried and mixed with sesame and sumac, otherwise it wouldn't taste good. My kids don't know the taste of bread baked with za'atar leaves on winter mornings but maybe if we find some za'atar here in Illinois, I'll find a recipe and make them that sort of bread.

On the way to the hills my father would tell stories that I loved to hear. He'd point to the trunks of the eucalyptus trees that my mother's uncle crashed into and the village of Jisr a-Zarka that was turned into a prison by the coastal highway. "Look," he'd say. "The only pretty village still left on the coast and look at what they did to it." He'd point to Damon Prison, where he sat for a full year, and tell us how cold it was there, though it was not from his lips that I heard how they would seat him on glass Coca-Cola bottles during interrogation and not from him that I heard how they'd stretch his body over a chair, hands tied to his feet all night long. "Look, there's the Damon," he would say, "Best friends I ever had were in there, best ones I'll ever have."

Later on, once we were in middle school, we no longer went za'atar picking, maybe because the hills were gone, and the za'atar was now grown in hothouses and was different — bigger, with wider and sadder leaves and with the taste of decay.

Yes, I must go out on a drive with the kids. I'll check where people take their kids around here and we'll go there.

Maybe Palestine will join, and if the weather is good I'll open the windows so that the air whips our faces. I'll want to tell them a story during the drive, a story that they won't forget, to point at something and unravel a yarn, but I won't find a single memory to unravel.

4

I always arrive ahead of time when picking the kids up from school. First, I wait for my eldest on a side street close to her junior high, even though there's plenty of parking, owing to the fact that I am there early and our car is the smallest and cheapest of all the family cars. My daughter has never said anything, but I prefer to wait for her here, away from the other students, so that the car does not embarrass her. When I ask her if she's getting along okay, she nods.

When she was little, the only stories my daughter heard were read from Hebrew books at bedtime. Sometimes I told her about kings and pretty princesses and knights galloping on fearsome horses, scabbards filled with golden swords. But when she went to kindergarten and started to ask questions about our lives, we taught her that not every question has an answer and that the past is sometimes best forgotten in the service of the future. And when the kids in her class would talk about their grandmas and grandpas we told her that not everyone has those. During her first Holocaust Remembrance Day, she decided that her grandma and grandpa had been killed in the Holocaust, and we said nothing. And on Memorial Day, a short while later, she asked if her grandparents had been killed in a war. She heard Arabic spoken at home but never said a word in that language. She knew at kindergarten they spoke one language and at home a different one, and she was sure that this was the way of the world, one language for the home and one for the outside world, similar and yet so different. In third grade a teacher told her that she was Druze, and my daughter thought the word was a curse. In fourth grade she heard from a classmate that she is an Arab, and at home she inquired about the significance of the word. Some people are born Arabs we told her, and some are born Jews.

Our daughter got older and became aware that she was different. She heard on the news about war, about Palestine, about a national home, and she understood that she had no choice but to choose a side, like everyone else. In the Arabic that she understood but did not speak, I told her that she is Palestinian, and that Palestine was ruined, and that she won't find it on a map in geography class, that she'll have to imagine Palestine, as I do, from the stories I'd heard or the stories that I tell her and myself. In Arabic I told her secrets she must not reveal. There are answers that can be given only in one language, and when they come off the tongue in a different language they take on a different significance, sometimes the opposite. And what happens if you give the right answer in the wrong language to the angels that visit the graves right after burial and ask for answers to the questions that determine whether you, the newly perished soul, will reside eternally in heaven or hell? Are you then also considered an infidel and battered down into the void or are you embraced as a believer and granted tranquility in your grave?

In Hebrew we told her that she is a citizen, with equal rights. An answer she knew to recite even if she didn't understand it.

My daughter was a quiet baby. When she was born I didn't hear her wail. And only when the midwife came out to the waiting room and said mazel tov and I walked into the delivery room did I hear her soft crying and her mother's, who took her, swaddled in Hadassah Medical Center blankets, in her arms. The two cried together and were calmed as one.

My wife did not let me touch my daughter on the day she was born. I just looked at her, lying in one of those clear plastic boxes in the row of newborns, and I watched the nurse hold her naked body in her left hand while, with her right hand, she washed her under the faucet. I could have then shown the nurses my hospital bracelet, which proved that I was the father and allowed me to pick her up in my arms, hug her, whisper to her that I love her, but I waited for the okay from Palestine, which came the day after the birth when she handed me the infant, her expression making it clear to me that she knew there was no other way.

After two days in the hospital we took a taxi to the fourth-floor apartment we were renting on Guatemala Street. We'd moved in as soon as we found out that Palestine was pregnant, one month after the wedding. We borrowed a crib from the newsroom secretary, whose kids were already grown. The stroller and the portable infant car seat came from the health reporter's niece. A neighbor, whose name we never knew, gave us clothes, from zero to twelve months.

At first my wife thought that she was late for her period because of stress, but after a few bouts of morning sickness and finding two red lines on the pregnancy test that she had me buy for her at the pharmacy in French Hill, we went to the doctor who determined that my wife was in her thirteenth week of pregnancy.

Not a soul could know. Not yet, it was too soon, too dangerous.

There's no shortage of busybodies among the Arab student population and I didn't want any of them to notice and send word home, where the news would quickly and surely reach Tira. I dropped out of university and we rented an apartment in Kiryat HaYovel, one I could not afford on the basis of my freelance work. I let the editor in chief of the paper know that I had left school and that I was available for a full-time position, hoping that he'd sign me to a contract and provide a steady job with benefits, even if the salary was low. However, I soon learned from the longtime reporters at the paper that the only way to get a contract was to deliver a slew of egregiously wordy stories, because freelancers are paid by the word and only once it makes no fiscal sense for the paper to pay per word is a staff position finally made available. Aside from the arts pieces I filed, I started wandering around the West Bank and Gaza, picking up material and reporting it, and within six months I was the paper's West Bank reporter, with a minimum wage salary. Half of it went straight to rent. My friends at the paper told me that the only way to get a bump in salary would be to present a competing offer from a rival paper, at which point the editor in chief would match that offer. The offer came with the outbreak of yet another war, at a time when I was one of the only reporters willing to walk out into the killing zones and deliver the goods that the Israeli press demanded.

❖   ❖   ❖

We named our daughter Yasmin, a name that works in both
Hebrew and Arabic, and I changed the family name on the
identity card to Hadad, even though I kept the name I inherited from my father on my bylines. During the first year
of her life my daughter's crib was in her mother's bedroom
while I slept on a mattress on the floor of the other room,
as I had been ever since our move. Palestine stayed home
with Yasmin until she was one year old, and aside from
trips to the well-baby clinic and the occasional outing to the
doctor's office, they did not leave the house, at first because
we were scared of germs and viruses and later because we
were scared of her being injured in the war.

Palestine was changed after the birth. As soon as she
was discharged from the hospital she started studying, preparing for her university entrance exams. Six months later
she enrolled in the school of social work. And when our
daughter was one year old she asked that Yasmin be moved
to the room in which I slept, and she moved me into her bed.
Without preamble, and perhaps simply on account of the
intimacy of a shared bed, Palestine and I slept together for
the first time. I was filled with a great joy, and she at first
would cry, and then she stopped. When Palestine began
university, we'd leave Yasmin with a neighbor who looked
after three babies in an unregistered day care in her home.
She's really advanced, the day care owner said, unaware of
the fact that we'd added two months to her birthdate when
we filled out the registration form.

Yasmin never heard a word about Tira from Palestine
or me, though from time to time she would ask if there was

such a thing as a blood relative. Sometimes I wonder if the kids have heard of Tira, perhaps on the news or from friends or in their studies.

I watch my daughter as she leaves school and hope to see her chatting with some of the other kids on the way to the car, only to see, yet again, that she's walking alone, eyes downcast. She has never been at a friend's house and every once in a while I ask my wife, who says no she has not asked to invite anyone over to hers. It's possible Yasmin doesn't invite anyone over because she is nervous that they'll pick up on our strange family dynamic. After all, in Jerusalem, as soon as she was old enough to understand that she should not understand, she stopped hosting. When she asked questions and we failed to provide clear answers, she stopped accepting friends' invitations to come over. What does she say in this part of the world when she's asked where she's from, what her religion is, who she is? Can "I don't know" be considered a correct answer to the question: "Which God do you believe in?" Is "I don't have one" an acceptable response to the question: "What is your nationality?"

I always arrive on time to pick the boys up from elementary school. On wintry days the cars pull up outside in a row and the school principal, in a heavy coat, scarf, and earmuffs, holds a walkie-talkie in his hand and calls out the names of the kids according to the signs pinned to the sun visors on the cars. I always turn down the sun visor with the note that bears my older son's name, even though after a few weeks the principal already recognized the car. He also knew that the older brother comes out with the younger one, holding

148 Sayed Kashua

his hand and leading him from the school to the row of cars out front. When it's freezing, the best way to protect the kids from overexposure to cold is to wait for the principal to wave them forward out of the heated school and into the car.

The kids have abandoned Hebrew and now speak only in English among themselves. The boys, no longer hearing the language in school and on TV, have forgotten it entirely. Back in Jerusalem, the little guy never even spoke to us in Arabic. He just understood what was said and responded in Hebrew, the language of his day care. Here, within a few months, he started responding in English.

"Dad," my middle son asked me a few months after school began. "Are we Muslim?"

"Why?"

"No reason," he said. "Just wanted to know." Then at the parent-teacher conference halfway through the year his homeroom teacher praised his newfound command of English, a language in which he knew not a single word at the start of the year, and reminded me of how scared I was at the onset, on the first day of school, when all I could think of was how would the kids tell the teacher that they needed to go the bathroom? "His English has gotten remarkably better," the cheery teacher said, adding that socially, too, he was doing well and that in the afternoons he went off with his Muslim friends to go pray in one of the classrooms. The kid hadn't said anything about prayers, and when I gently inquired if he even knows how to pray he replied that he had learned by watching the other kids. He did not pray at home—no one did—and he steadfastly refused to answer any of the questions I asked about the prayer services and his Muslim friends, saying only that this was how it was in school, that he was one of the Muslims and the Muslims went to pray. And Dad, enough, I don't want to talk about it, so I stopped pushing.

"There are some questions that have no answers," is what his sister said.

Americans eat dinner at six in the evening, but my kids are hungry right after school, which ends at three thirty, so at four I serve them a dish that I cook up in the university dorm. Only once I got here did I start cooking in earnest, searching, for the first time, for recipes for the sort of simple down-home dishes my mother used to make. Rice is the base and you add green beans or white beans, potatoes, and black-eyed peas and cook it all up with a cut of meat and tomato sauce. Molokhiyeh leaves, which are prepared without sauce, are impossible to find here. And I really wanted to make my kids a great green bowl of molokhiyeh, and I really wanted to have some myself. But in order to get dried molokhiyeh leaves one has to drive to the outskirts of Chicago, where, I was told, there's an Arab neighborhood, mostly Palestinian, and one can get anything, just like in the old country, in the village, in East Jerusalem.

Once a week I stop and let the kids get fast food. Sometimes we go inside and sometimes we stay in the car, ordering at the drive-through. They love American food, especially the boys, who prefer fast food to homemade dishes.

Palestine usually finishes work at five. When the weather is nice she walks home, but during the endless winter I ask my daughter to watch her little brothers and I drive to pick her up, waiting as close to the building as possible.

At seven in the evening the boys take their bath, and at seven thirty they go to bed. I don't read them bedtime stories like I used to. The big one already reads to himself and the little one, who loved the stories I used to read to him, now reads himself bedtime stories in English on the iPad. Still, I sit beside my son in bed until the iPad finishes telling the story, and then I give him a kiss and tuck the blanket around him. The kids' rooms are not decorated. There are no pictures or posters on the doors or the walls, and that is true of all the rooms of the house in which my wife and kids live and the dorm room in which I spend most of my time. We are careful not to leave any marks, because you never know when it'll be time to get up and go.

5

I'll invite Palestine out to dinner. Just the two of us, no kids.
I'll wear the button-down checked shirt I got at the giant
outlet store a half-hour's drive from where we live. A shirt
with the logo of a polo player on horseback, which was on
sale, like all of the clothes at that store, and cost around ten
dollars. That was the shirt I wore when I boarded the plane
to Tel Aviv and in which I arrived at the hospital, so that
they would see that I have a shirt with a designer logo that
the residents of Tira appreciate, a shirt that would leave
my family members with the impression that I've made it.
Palestine liked the shirt. When I came out of the changing
room, ostensibly without having looked at my reflection in
the mirror, even though there was one in the room, she said
to me: "That shirt fits you just right," and her words made
me so happy. It was one of the few sentences she said to me
over the years, deliberately or not, and I cradled it inside me.

Yes, I'll invite her to dinner. The kids can stay home. Yasmin
is old enough to watch over her brothers, or maybe, just to
be on the safe side, I'll suggest we get a babysitter, for the
first time. I'll take her to Picasso, the restaurant with the best
rating in town, according to the internet. I checked the menu
and the prices aren't all that bad. We'll drink red wine — I

already know which label I'll choose — and the bottle won't cost more than twenty dollars. I'll inquire as to whether she might be interested in one of the fish courses, in which case I'll suggest a white in a similar price range. I'll make do with a first course. I don't like feeling stuffed and anyway I don't like eating too much when I'm drinking.

Sometimes I think that I ought to start everything from the beginning. I'll write short little love notes in Arabic, handwritten, preferably in pencil, as the students do. Love letters on lined paper or graph paper, like in school. Love letters that have been torn out of notebooks. I never once wrote a love letter, even though my classmates all did. I didn't know how they got the courage to send them off to the girls. I knew that Arabic had set sentences and rhymes that you used in your first letters and that if the girl responded with letters of her own, showing an interest in furthering the relationship, then the character of the letters could change, morphing into something more personal.

I didn't have the courage to send love letters and I didn't have anyone to send them to. Over the years I've wondered what would have happened had I been a letter writer, and I was sorry that I had not taken part in that rite of youth. Did Palestine's husband once send her love letters? I'd ask myself that every now and again, in moments of jealousy that I didn't fully comprehend. And if he did, when did he start? How old was she when he sent her his first letter? And what did it say? Was he a gifted writer, who, for practical purposes, decided to pursue a career in accounting? Was he a better writer than me? How did his letters make her feel and in what ways did she choose to reply? Where did he first see her, and when? Sometimes I imagine a girl in

junior high standing by a window in her house, looking out
to the street, waiting to see her beloved, who would pass by
at a chosen hour, and she, perhaps, placing her palm on the
window pane, smiling, promising with her eyes that she will
wait for him until it is permissible, until she is of age, until
they can be together. She will wait for an eternity if that is
what's required.

Sometimes I think to myself that if their love was so
strong he wouldn't have given up on her so easily, merely
on account of a short story printed in a student journal in
Hebrew, followed by a rumor that buzzed through the village. Their love, if it had been true, would have endured
and overcome, and they would have kept it alive even at the
price of moving from their house, no matter how luxurious
it may have been, to a different city, a different country, far
from the evil tongues of the village. But that didn't happen.
Is jealousy stronger than love? Does suspicion, once it's been
seeded in the heart, feed off love's roots? I don't know who
made the decision about separation; Palestine never talked
about her husband and never said a word about what had
happened. And I didn't ask. What right did I have to ask?

Maybe their love never faded, and though they were forced
to consent to the dissolution of their marriage, they still,
nonetheless, loved one another with all their hearts? Sometimes I imagine her getting letters torn out of school notebooks, the pages filled with lines that bring her great joy and
terrible sorrow. What if she stayed in touch with her beloved
husband? What if they carried on meeting in secret corners
of Jerusalem and even continued to meet here, in Illinois?

Maybe I just need to be straight and to the point with Palestine, start everything anew like my father said, start over with the wife I've been married to for the past fourteen years. I'll invite her to dinner and tell her that I love her and that I want to go back to living with her and the children. That she must love me as I love her and then we'll go back to being a family the way we learned families ought to be. If she does not respond, I'll be assertive, saying that I've had it with the guilt. I'll be decisive. I'll say that just like her I am a victim, and at least I'm trying, fourteen straight years of trying, and I can't go on like this. I'm approaching forty and how long can I possibly wait to be forgiven? If she refuses, then I'll say I want to go back, take the kids and go back to Jerusalem, because there's nothing for me here. And I have absolutely nothing to do besides wait for the kids to finish their school days and drive them home and be with them until they climb into bed. I'll tell her that the hours alone are crushing me, shattering me, and that without the kids around I feel as though I'm dying, and at times I even wish for my own death. I'm sick of it all, I'll tell her. After all I didn't do anything on purpose, and I, too, deserve to at least once experience the taste of love. I don't mind being disappointed or discovering that in fact it is not true love. At least that way I can say I tried; I experienced. If she asks if in Jerusalem I felt less deadened, I'll lie and say yes, that at least there I knew the names of the barber and the grocer and two of the regular bartenders and I'd shop at the same butcher and ride on buses and in cars and would be able to look at the people and hazard a guess as to what they do and where they live. Here in Illinois I've been going to the barber once a month for over two years now,

and each time he greets me with a smile and asks if I've been
in before and then taps my name into the computer, which
tells him the sort of haircut I like. Here I go into the same
grocery store and get the same pack of Marlboro Lights
every other day and the people at the register never look at
me with an expression that risks conveying any sort of previ-
ous acquaintance. And if she says that the kids' futures are
brighter in the United States, I can agree and say that while
she may be right, that is also the reason I want to move to
a different city, a real city, where I won't be the only lonely
person, where there are gathering places for people like
me. A city with pubs and bars, plays, movie theaters, and
concerts, a city in which I have a chance of finding someone
I can love and who might love me. Palestine won't be jealous. She'll know that I would never dare put any distance
between myself and the kids, that I lack the courage, and
that no matter what I say, in the end, I'll do exactly as she
dictates, just as I've done throughout the years. But she
has not cast me off just yet, and maybe that's a good sign?
She has not cast me off, even though she no longer needs
me. Ever since we moved I have not worked and have no
way of making a living; I live in the dorm that she provides,
rented under her name and paid for by her monthly salary.
Maybe she's keeping me around for the kids? And perhaps
when they grow up and leave the house she'll ask that I
stop coming around? Sometimes I think the time has come
to find a job. After all, the visa given to visiting academics
allows for lawful employment in the United States for both
married partners. After all, even dishwashing or working the
register at one of the gas station convenience stores is better
than the empty hours of waiting. And maybe, if I found a

job, I'd also acquire the language and learn the local habits, bond with people, find friends who would invite me over to watch baseball games or to share family meals during the holidays, grilling up burgers and hotdogs and ears of corn.

Sometimes, when I'm alone in the dorm and waiting for the hour at which I go and pick up the kids, I imagine that I've published a book and an important TV host buys the book by mistake. She can't even remember how it was that the book wound up on her bedside table, but once she starts reading the fascinating work written by the author whose name she doesn't even know, she is incapable of stopping. And she invites me on to her show, because she'll never be able to forgive herself if she doesn't do everything in her power to convince her audience to read the wonderful book that changed all that she thought she knew about love, politics, loneliness, and family life. And I'll come on the show, and I'll be bashful and smart and modest, and I'll know that my kids are watching, and they're calling their mother. But she won't come. And I'll win important prizes, the names of which I don't know, and maybe even the Nobel, even though it isn't awarded for a single book but for a body of work. But maybe they'll change the rules and I'll be the first Palestinian writer to win it, and the Palestinians will be proud, and in Tira they will at long last believe that I'm a writer and not a gossiper looking to ruin the lives of others. Maybe then we'll be able to go home, take the kids and go back to Tira, and Palestine will be returned to the soil from which I uprooted her, and she will forgive me wholeheartedly and will hug me hard and whisper in my ear that she loves me, that she always has, but that her tongue has been tied ever since she left Tira.

* * *

Yes, I'll ask her out on a date, as they say around here. I'll use that word, "date," when I ask. I'll say it with a smile, like a sort of joke, so that she won't turn me down or be taken aback. And maybe I'll tell her about the first time I saw her, on the day of our wedding, and the feeling in me that was awakened by her presence. Though maybe it wouldn't be fair or right to remind her of that day, one of the most difficult days of her life. If that's the case, then where will I begin?

I considered lines that I must have heard on TV or in movies: "Let's talk about us, about the here and now." Or: "Let's turn over a new leaf, a new beginning." And maybe I'll apologize again, even though I've spoken a million apologies, especially during the early months, and she never once responded to my requests, asking only: "For what?" And I did not say: "For the story, for unintentionally inserting your name, that I didn't know of your existence, and I never had any intention of hurting you." But in the face of her suffering, "sorry" was the only word that escaped my lips—and she did, and still does, suffer, and each time my eyes meet hers I feel the need to beg for forgiveness. And with the years my guilt has intensified, and I don't know when it was that I stopped treating myself as yet another victim in the story, which was forced not only on her but on me, too. I don't know when I started feeling like I was a monster, believing with every bone in my body that I wrote the story about Palestine with clear and premeditated intent. When did I internalize the notion that all I had sought was to harm Palestine, to tarnish her honor and her family name, that I published a story with the clear goal of separating her from her husband because I desired to have her as my own. And because she did not respond to my courtship, I, therefore, decided to take revenge on her, ruin her house, soil her name, trample her honor, and leave her with no other choice?

~~Maybe I will tell her that I always loved her, even though I never dared to send her love letters. I'll tell her the truth that has been branded into me over the years, that I could not bear the thought of her living alongside another man, the notion that she was capable of loving someone other than me and as a result of that pain I did something cruel, something I knew would leave her with no other option? I'll tell her that I always loved her even though I never said a word about it, and I'll tell her that every single night I dream the story that I wrote, and that I've imagined the two of us making love ever since I imagined her existence. And that the story that wasn't has become an inseparable and uniquely fertile part of my memory. I'll ask her to dinner and I'll ask her for forgiveness, and if she asks for what, I'll tell her all of this, and I'll confess for the first time to a sin that I regretted not having sinned and will ask for absolution.~~

E

1

To the left of my father's bed, beneath a window that has never been opened, lay an Arab man of my age, who had come to the hospital on account of chest pains. The tests showed that everything was in order, but the doctors insisted on keeping him in for monitoring. His wife cried when he asked her to go home and spend the night with the kids. Judging by their accents, they were from Taybeh.

To my father's right was an older Jewish man who didn't speak a word and was visited by no one. I tugged the curtain closed around us and wished the Arab man a speedy recovery and said good night to the Jewish man. Jews and Arabs are still hospitalized side by side, as though stating that diseases and death are still to be shared experiences. Births, the delivery of life, are segregated with separate rooms for Arabs and Jews.

"You haven't been to the house," my father stated.

No, not yet. I'll go tomorrow.

Okay. Tell me more about your kids.

My kids, they're cute. They're smart. Pretty and handsome. Like I told you.

Remind me of their names.

The eldest one we called Yasmin.

Yasmin. Nice, Yasmin. I can see she is tall in the picture.

Tallest in her grade.

What grade is she in? Sorry, it's just hard for me to talk.

She's in junior high, eighth grade. Next year she'll already go to high school, because high school in America starts in ninth grade rather than tenth. Dad, you don't have to talk if it's hard for you.

And what's the name of the little rascal, the one with the curls?

Adam. He really is a little rascal. He's in kindergarten, five years old, and he speaks English like an American. And Amir's ten, in fifth grade.

Do they know they have a family? That they have a grandfather?

I don't know.

Your wife is very pretty.

Yes.

What do you tell the kids?

I haven't decided yet what to tell them and what not to tell them.

And what do you tell yourself?

I don't know. I just have the beginnings of stories but not the whole tale. I haven't yet found my ending.

Are you still the victim in these stories?

At that moment I discovered that as opposed to what many people think, new childhood memories can suddenly appear, and they are not just a dwindling collection of memories that are sealed at a certain stage, incapable of further expansion. All of a sudden, I was taken back to a holiday morning near my house. There's a pistol in my hand, and I see a little kid, roughly my age, who used to come around the neighborhood and visit his mother's relatives on holidays. Only on holidays did we get toy pistols that you could load with round red caps. Only on holidays did we get a stash of caps, more than was needed, because something in the mechanism of the pistol gave out after a few days anyway, usually by the end of the break, as though it knew the length of our holidays and vacations. I'd look at him, at that little kid, with his combed hair and his holiday finery — so much finer than our clothes — and be jealous of him. At times it seemed to me that I was envious of all the kids who didn't live in our neighborhood, all those from faraway, from rich and stately surroundings, who attended better schools, wore fancier clothes, and had bigger cars and different parents.

I remember that kid's mom, who seemed young and beautiful to me, though I can't retrieve her face from the depths of my memory but merely the cadence of her walk and the motion of her lips when she spoke to me. He was a handsome kid, like the kids from the good families in Egyptian movies. All I wanted was to impress him as he strode toward his relatives' house that morning, to make him look at me for once, at me and my cap gun and the cap rings I'd bought with the holiday allowance my grandmother had given me, because our parents never gave us money, only bought us new clothes and cap guns. I fired the gun in order to get the attention of the kid who never once looked in my direction; in his honor I fired off an entire eight-cap ring, and I was lucky because they all went off and weren't old and malfunctioning as they sometimes were, making hardly any noise, the gunpowder having seeped out of the cap before it was even all loaded up. And instead of seeing the handsome kid that I was trying to impress look up and smile—and ask if he could shoot the gun, too—he stood still, pressed his palms against his ears, as though trying to crush his head, and started screaming in a way I'd never heard a kid scream. Afterward he sat down on the sand in the middle of the street. I saw his mother rush out and try to soothe him and then saw some of her relatives come outside and escort the kid into their house. I stood there, bristling, unmoving, and said nothing as the scene unfolded around me. His mother was wearing a long, pleated skirt and had pretty sandals on her feet, and she walked toward me confidently. I was not afraid, or maybe I was just paralyzed by the shock. Her lips were painted red and I watched their delicate movements as she asked me not to fire the gun because her son is afraid of loud noises, because he is a special child.

When she turned away, I was left with the humiliation of knowing that I am not special, and deep down inside I swore that come the next holiday, I would be waiting for him again, with a gun.

You didn't answer.
Which question?
I asked who the victim is in your stories.
I'm still undecided.
I wanted to tell my father how the power to shape a story was scary to me, nearly paralyzing. From the moment

the client decided that I would write his story, I felt like his fate was in my hands; his legacy dependent on my imagination and memory.

The fears began to surface with the fifth book that I authored. The client, whose sons had hired my writing services, was a healthy seventy-year-old woman who could tell wonderful children's stories that she had heard from her grandmother—and the kids, whose lives had been enriched by those stories, tried to publish a book of her stories about ghosts and goblins that abduct children and the village wise man or the particularly clever kid who was able to trick the goblin and slay the evil monster. But they said that no publisher was willing to take them or their mother's tales seriously. They wanted the stories collected and bound, preserved in the unique way that their mother told them, so that they could be passed on to their grandchildren and their grandchildren's grandchildren, because somehow, not one of the girls in the family inherited the narrative gift that was passed down in the family from woman to woman. They knew the plots, but their narration they felt ruined it all. "It has to be in her words," I remember her eldest son saying to me on the day that I first interviewed the woman and recorded her. She was a pleasant woman, quick to laugh, though with nothing notably unique in the way she told stories of goblins and flying carpets and winged wolves that slaughtered the sheep in sleepy villages. She did flap her hands, pause occasionally as parents do when reading bedtime stories to their children, make the sound effects of slaps and explosions as necessary, but it was in essence the look in her eye that her daughters had not inherited, the look of a small child telling the story as she heard it for the first time. I opened the book of her stories with an intro about Jerusalem, the city in which she, like her mother and grandmother, was raised. Her stories of childhood were pleasant and warm and there was virtually no need to edit them, aside from the ones that took place during the war years. There she told of how the Arab neighbors turned on her family, going from warmhearted characters to cold-blooded killers. I corrected her in the pages of the book and wrote instead of an enduring neighborliness, of people caring for one another even during a time of war, and I added that she still thinks of her Arab neighbors and sometimes she still picks up the scent of fresh pita being baked with za'atar on the Friday mornings before the war, a scent that makes her wonder if they're still telling the same stories she once heard or if the tales disappeared, too, along with everything else. And her son, who swore he'd read the whole book to her and praised the work I'd done, said nothing beyond thank you. Two days after the thirty copies of the book arrived at the family home, a picture of a woman with an engaging, kind gaze on the cover and the title that her children had chosen, *The Folk Tales of Grandma Miriam*, I got a message from the eldest son, who informed me that his mother had died, and he just wanted to let me know how happy and excited she had been by the publication of the book.

The woman was healthy, and the firstborn son, whom I met at the Shiva, said her passing had been a complete surprise, that she simply had not woken up and that her daughter had found her in bed with a smile on her lips and an unmoving heart.

The doctors, who found no reason to conduct an autopsy, said it had been a heart attack, and I was afraid that it had happened because of me, because at the very moment of her death, during precisely that same hour of the morning, I had erased the two tapes, recording over the spools on which her life story had been held.

2

"He didn't mean it. Don't take it too hard. He's your older brother, and he'll always be your older brother, and the things he said were not said from the heart, believe me. They were spoken in anger. You don't know what we went through because of that small patch of land that we still have. You don't know what he had to go through because of it and still does. And not just him, all of us. You think your father got sick for no reason? They broke his heart, and now all of the weight is on your brothers' shoulders, especially his. And you don't know. You left and detached yourself from the troubles. And maybe it's best that way, maybe it's for the best that you were far away.

The people closest to you, or the people you thought were close, they're the ones who swoop down on you when you're weak, who want to tear at your flesh while you're still alive. After all, there was barely space to build houses for your brothers, and when I think about the grandchildren . . . I'd rather not think about it. Where will they go? Where will they build houses and where will they live? Even the little that remains they want to take. The people that I could once turn to in my hour of need have now become the source of trouble, and of course nothing is officially documented, nothing is written down, and nothing can be. What were once agreements and signatures are no longer valid, and in order to reach a resolution every single one of the relatives, from 1948 up until now, has to sign off on it, and half of them are no longer on speaking terms. Brothers have become enemies, quarreling over every square foot of earth, trampling the weak. And what sort of strength do we have? And who even imagined we'd ever find ourselves in this situation, where the people with whom you once broke bread now yearn for your death and are willing to do whatever it takes in order to dispossess you from the little that you own.

And everyone is right, everyone is right, and nothing will convince them that they're mistaken. They're all certain that they've been terribly wronged, and no letters, no agreements, no land distribution claims signed by the older generation are going to convince them otherwise. And even the elders who, whether by pen or thumbprint, signed official documents before a lawyer, deny their signatures and fan the flames of anger among the younger generations. They have nowhere to build. Where could they build? And where will their kids go? So in their rage they prey on the weak, the helpless. And don't think they haven't taken. They've taken, they've taken already. And we thought that it was over and done and they signed new paperwork and shook hands and smiled and kissed your father and your brothers and said thank you and how wonderful it is that we can go back to being a family. But a few years down the road another family member turned up. And once he understood that we had succumbed one time, he thought maybe we'd do so again, until there's just nowhere for you to go. And when you have your back pressed up against the wall, you have no choice but to find the strength to fight.

You think your father fell ill for no reason? And you think your brother spoke that way for no reason? He should not have spoken to you the way he did. He would like to have you back among us more than anything else, but it was rage that spoke, the anger of feeling that he had been abandoned, that he had to endure all alone. Do you know that they opened fire on his house a few times while he and his wife were asleep, while his kids were asleep inside? But he didn't give in because where will his children go? For all that's left is barely enough for them to build houses on top of one another. Did you know that his wife left the house? Rightfully, out of fear, she took the kids and slept at her parents' house for three weeks. Who could blame her? And who could have imagined that your brothers, who work hard in order to raise their kids and get them the best possible education, would find themselves threatened in their own homes? Cursed is the soil, but what can be done? There's nowhere else to go. There's no choice.

In the name of God, don't be angry with him, and don't take it to heart. The only hope we have is the chance of seeing you reunited. I'm sorry that I'm crying. Seeing the two of you fight is devastating to me, the thought that even you, even you two would fight, that is something that never once crossed my mind. You'll see. He'll come back here and ask for forgiveness. I talked to him and he's already sorry about what he said and sad about having said those things; he didn't mean them. He only wants for you to be by his side, for him not to feel alone while waging this cursed war that was forced upon us and upon him.

And do you think that your father, once he heard that they're threatening his children and endangering the lives of his grandchildren, didn't want to give them everything they were asking for? He nearly went out of his mind. And what do you think? That what happened to him happened for no reason? And now they show up at the hospital as if their hands are clean, as if they were not the ones behind it all. Who could do such a thing but them? Only them, for it is all so clear. In the name of God, your brother does not have a dispute with anyone in this world. He goes from home to work and from work to the family and the kids. That's it. And then disaster occurs, a terrible disaster, and there's nowhere to run, nowhere to go. So it was only frustration coming from your brother's throat, and instead of speaking a word of longing he unwittingly spit out a stream of anger over the many years of absence.

He knows you won't come back, which is not to say that heaven forbid that's my preference. For you must know that it is my hope to see you among us again and to be granted the privilege of having your children grow up with their cousins in their natural environment. Though maybe the distance and the years have already made you used to a different life, and you might not want to make yourselves a home in Tira. Am I right? I wish I was wrong, but I am a mother and a mother is never wrong about her intuitions. Your brother knows deep down that you didn't come to claim land or an inheritance. He knows that very well. And I'm not saying that it isn't your right. Of course it is, even if there is only a little bit left it is still your right, even though you didn't fight and didn't stand beside your brothers to defend what remains. It does not detract from your lawful right. But your brother knows that you will ask for nothing, and I promised him that I know you well enough to know that it does not befit you to ask for your share, small though it may be. Who would ever believe that I would have to say things of this nature? Who would ever believe that I would be forced to mediate between children who were raised to always stand by each other's side? And he did stand by your side, in the face of the rumors and the slander, the vicious lies that were spread about you, and he held his ground courageously, as did your father. They sang your praises and assailed your accusers; even though it besmirched their honor, they never abated. It followed them everywhere. You don't know what they went through, as did I, yes, as did I. But I reckon that you can imagine, because you were always a smart kid, and the customs of this place are not foreign to you even if you've disregarded them.

He did not mean a word that he said. He is your older brother and he would give up his entire world for you and he will be coming this evening. He promised he will come, and you must promise me in the name of God that you will kiss his head, ask for his forgiveness, make clear that you are seeking nothing. And may God keep you, my son."

3

My father ordered a TV to the room. He can't live without the news. At home, too, the radio is constantly tuned in to a twenty-four-hour news station and is left on all night by the bed. My mother has gotten used to its drone.

In the hospital, for the price of thirty-five shekels per night, a TV rental service technician installed an old TV on an adjustable metal wall mount. "After the first week," the tech said, "the price goes down to twenty-five."

"Don't worry," Dad said. "I won't hang on for the discount."

My father donned earphones — "for a single payment of ten shekels" — and watched the news:

Israel Police first sergeant Erez Levi was killed today in a car-ramming attack in the village of Umm el-Hiran. The attack came in the midst of an operation to remove an illegal construction from a Bedouin village. He is survived by his wife and two children.

Minister of Public Security Gilad Erdan accuses the Arab MKs who took part in the protest rally: the policeman's blood is on your hands. The brother of the driver contends that after being shot the alleged assailant lost control of the vehicle.

The responsible parties will have to rule on this matter, not the officers in the field but the high-ranking officers that organized the operation.

In the military cemetery in Yavne First Sergeant Erez Levi, age thirty-four, is laid to rest after being killed by a car ramming while clearing illegal Bedouin buildings in Umm el-Hiran. The footage from a police helicopter shows the car driven by the local resident, Musa Abu el-Hiran. Excuse me, Yaaqub Abu el-Hiran, and here he is seen accelerating as the police officers fire in his direction. The Israel Police has determined today that it was a car-ramming attack, while the family contends that the collision occurred on account of a loss of control of the car during the shooting, and all this takes place on the heels of the decision to remove the residents from their homes in the unrecognized village.

The Members of Knesset from the Joint List of Arab parties took part in the protest rallies. Joint List chairman MK Ayman Odeh was wounded in the head. Correspondent Nir Dvori, you're there, in the field: all of this happened in the early morning, and since then I presume things have quieted down considerably?

That's right, Oren, and it should be noted that all is calm here right now, once the destruction of all fifteen buildings that the police intended to destroy has been completed, despite this grave incident and the murder of the police officer. Those developments delayed the time schedule of the police, but the mission was completed in the end.

I'd like to shift the camera, here, have a look, at what may be the first case of retaliation after the incident. Across the way from this small village, Umm el-Hiran, a Jewish village called Hiran is being built, the early infrastructure already visible on the ground. What you see over there is an equipment hangar for roadwork tools being used in the construction. And someone has already decided to torch that spot. It's unclear if that will be the last action taken here, as there's plenty of rage, a great deal of frustration, and we've seen it erupt a bit over the past several hours. But it must be said that even in the midst of this incident, we saw many young Bedouin residents of the area trying to calm things down, restrain, and they were the ones who prevented rocks from being thrown at the police. And another word, because this may be important as we move forward, there are preparations for the possibility of additional eruptions of rage and frustration in the near future. Many people are currently engaged in trying to lower the height of the flames, including the president of the country, who is speaking with Bedouin leaders and Arab mayors in order to soothe and to moderate, because they understand that this was an unusual incident, most grave, that could alter the shape of this landscape.

Nir, let's hear the reactions from Member of Knesset Ayman Odeh and from the police's deputy commander of the southern sector. Here they are:

I'm telling you that the bloodshed could have been avoided. Prime Minister Netanyahu, who has already marked the Arab population as enemy number one, made the brutal decision to ruin an entire village, to kick and pound children, women, and men.

There's no way to explain a situation like this by saying that he didn't see them. There were dozens of police officers moving in two rows in a very noticeable way. There is just no way that he did not see them, and whoever races out toward them at that sort of speed, on those road conditions, it is absolutely clear, has injurious intent, and he did make contact, and he killed police personnel deployed in the line of duty.

Nir, would you like to add another word?

Yes, we must add that the Bedouin Authority in the Negev conducted intense negotiations in order to try and move this unrecognized and illegal village to the nearby Bedouin town of Hura. Some of the families did move and some did not, stating that an adequate arrangement was not found for them. That is what we've been told by the residents here. And the police say that there is a signed order from the Supreme Court, a decision that cannot be changed, and that is why the decree stood and that is why they were sent to destroy the illegal houses here today.

Okay, thank you very much for now. Shalom to Member of Knesset Ahmad Tibi.

Shalom, Oren.

You are currently at Soroka Hospital in Beersheva, visiting Member of Knesset Isma Sa'adi.

Osama. Osama Sa'adi.

Osama Sa'adi, who was injured. Look, Minister Erdan says that Ayman Odeh and the rest of the MKs from the Joint List arrived in order to fan the flames, that his blood is also on your hands, and that you are a disgrace to the state of Israel. Here on the screen we have what he posted on Facebook today, what do you have to say to that?

4

The nurse helps me transfer Dad into a wheelchair. His legs can't support him, but his arms have retained some of their strength. "It's humiliating," he tells the nurse when he asks for a wheelchair in order to go the bathroom. The catheter is still connected to his body, and the nurse hangs it from the wheelchair and shows me how to transport him.

"Take me outside, my son," my father ordered. "I'm suffocating in here."

"But it's not allowed," I said. "They specifically said that you are not allowed out."

I pushed the wheelchair out of the dark room. The Jewish patient was awake, staring at the ceiling. The Russian nurse on the night shift nodded at me when I looked to her for approval.

"You'll be cold," I told my father, and he did not respond.

"Maybe I should take a sheet?" I asked him, and he said no, he'd actually welcome a bit of cold.

"But they specifically said that we have to be careful that you not catch any sort of infectious diseases, Dad. They asked that relatives with a cold not come and visit, because this is the season and —

"Right, and that's why they put me in the infectious diseases department. I need to get out."

The elevator arrived at our floor and the doors pinged open. There was no one in the waiting area.

"What time is it anyway?"

"Midnight," I told my father as I pushed him into the elevator.

On the way out, a young man sat alone on a bench outside the closed café and peered into his cell phone. He raised his head as we walked past, but his blank expression said nothing.

"It's cold, Dad," I said as the automatic glass door opened.

"Actually, it's nice," he said, and I imagined him smiling as he used to do when Mom would complain about the cold and he would insist on pushing the TV into the yard to watch the soccer matches in the fresh air. "We'll make it feel like the stadium here," he'd say. "Do you have any idea how cold it is in Manchester?"

And once every four years, when the World Cup came around, always during the summer, the TV would stay outdoors for the duration of the tournament and relatives and neighbors would gather round and watch. I loved the World Cup so much when I was little because my father loved it, and I waited for the Olympics, too, because my father waited for them. A pleasant memory of watching together, a feeling of excitement and anticipation, which I reproduced in the life story of a kibbutz member who had fled Argentina after being hounded by the authorities for his membership in a left-wing underground association. All he had told me about was the underground, the flight, and the escape to Israel in 1982. And that was the year of the first World Cup I remembered: my father so wanted Algeria to win, and the Spanish hosts had an anthropomorphized orange as their mascot, and kids collected cards with pictures of the players.

Give me a cigarette.

I passed him one and sat down beside him on the bench.

Polite kid. You don't smoke next to your father?

No. I just don't feel like having a cigarette.

Did you know that your grandmother bought me a pack of cigarettes when I was twelve?

No. Why?

Just did. She walked into the house and gave me the cigarettes. You have to start smoking, she commanded. You have to be a man.

Well, once it was . . .

Ever since I can remember myself she wanted me to be a man, because you need to have a man in the family to defend it, to defend it after your grandfather has been killed. Sometimes I think that she was just telling tales, that there was no war, and that you never had a grandfather and I never had a father. He laughed and exhaled the cigarette smoke, "man."

Dad.

You say "dad" a lot.

Can I please come home?

Can you?

What's changed since I left?

You tell me.

❊   ❊   ❊

Me? I left. How would I know? And yet I know everything, because I've imagined Tira every day since, guessing who's married to whom, who's built a new house, who's died early, who's been born.

Every day I sketched the map anew, walking home from elementary school and from there to middle school and high school. I stood on the roof and looked around, and I saw how the few remaining fields gave way to garages and shops and carpentry workshops. How houses replaced vineyards, storage units instead of guava trees, a Shabbat market where the fig trees once stood. I left but I kept harvesting information, and when there was no information for me to reap, I simply made it up. I didn't for a second stop searching for the signs that would explain my departure, which was, after all, forced upon me. Or did I force it upon myself? The end of the story with the house was foretold, and I assembled the plot details accordingly. I determined at the outset that there was nowhere to return to, that no matter how much I might want to return, the path would be blocked by coils of barbed wire, guard towers, and military dogs with bared teeth that could tear my flesh.

And I wanted to return and still do, and I know all too well that I have no other place in this world to run to, no alternative shelter in which I can ensconce myself, start a family, and raise kids. I will always be on the lookout for warning signs, everywhere, in every bit of news, clues that fit into the larger picture that I've drawn in my mind. Yes, I still am the victim in the stories that I tell myself, and how could I not be?

Look, Dad, it isn't just Tira, and how could I be like you, full of pride and fighting spirit? Look around, Dad.

I'm not making this up. There are no mirages shimmering in front of me. I will never be a warrior, Dad, and I will always be embarrassed by my vulnerability. I wish I could be otherwise, but I'm too cowardly, and I've swapped my war for stories. But are they not true stories? What could I have done with no weapon at my disposal? Even if there was, I no longer know in which direction to point its muzzle, and for some reason every time I imagine a battle before sleep, it ends with my rifle pressed up against my temple. I don't know the identity of the enemy or which flag the allies are flying. The war games that I conjure always end in my death. Yet every night I am prepared to sacrifice myself anew, even though I no longer know for what or for whom. Yes, it's a shameful surrender. I know. You don't have to tell me that. How jealous I was of you when you told us that as kids you always knew precisely who your enemies were, that you had no doubt that your dreams would soon be realized. And now, Dad, what do you think now? Can you forgive me for wearing a white flag on my lapel, a flag that I've pinned to the sleeves of my children, too, as soon as they were swaddled, at birth, in hospital blankets?

By God, Dad, I'm trying, trying to gather the courage, trying to remember your words, which do not relent and continue to sear like the bark-stripped branches of the lemon tree. And I can no longer find in me the strength, am incapable of convincing myself of struggle for the sake of struggle rather than the outright pursuit of victory. I cannot understand the significance of pride, cannot internalize the meaning of honor, of which you spoke during all those years. Only the power of flight and defeat can I comprehend.

Do you remember all the songs you used to play for us, Dad? Do you remember the music you used to play in the car when we'd go pick za'atar after the rains? Songs that all started with pain, with banishment, suffering, songs that spoke of shackles, handcuffs, prison cells, and confinement chambers? The music was sad at first, sobbing the way only an oud can, and then in the end it would shift and the singers would promise victory and redemption, the release of prisoners, swearing the shackles would melt away. Do you remember, Dad, how at the end of the song the darkness would subside, how they'd promise that the sun would shine, the light would come pouring down, and the wilted flowers would bloom again?

I don't remember.

How could you not remember?

Remind me.

Where do you want me to start?

From the beginning.

Where does the beginning begin?

I'm thirsty.

We'll go up to the room, Dad.

You're saying "dad" a lot.

Tell me something I don't know.

You want an end to your story?

I want a beginning.

Do you remember the rain that came down that day? The silence of the drive? There was no music in the car, and I did not tell any tale on the way to the bus stop. Only the sound of the rain that I loved so much up until that drive, and all the way I thought of nothing. I was not angry with you for the story that you wrote or the ruin that you brought.

I did not think of what they would say in the village and about whether or not a day would come when your wife would forgive you and you would have children and a family. Throughout the drive I was angry because I hated the tapping of the rain. I started to hate the rain that I waited for all year, every year. And do you know what was scary, my beloved son? The scariest thing in the world was that at that moment I longed for your death.

5

At 6:00 a.m., I strode down Kfar Saba's main street, dragging my little suitcase behind me. It used to take fifteen minutes to walk from the share taxi stand outside the hospital to the row of bus stops along the Ra'anana–Kfar Saba Junction. I didn't know when the buses started running. My mother was likely making her way to the hospital with one of my brothers. They must have called her; the nurse said they usually make the calls in the morning. The ring of the phone interrupting the rhythm of her heart as she hurried to answer, and they asked if they were speaking with Mrs. the-appropriate-last-name, and she answered that, yes, she was speaking, and maybe she was already crying before she even said yes.

It is not going to rain today. I didn't need to check the forecast to know. Kfar Saba's main drag looks just as I remembered from my last walk. I always stopped at red lights at the pedestrian crossings. They were the same — and the streets were still empty at this early hour of the morning.

Wednesday? I think it's already Wednesday. An ordinary Wednesday. In Illinois, it's ten at night. The boys are surely already asleep, and my daughter is holed up in her room while Palestine is probably reading in bed. I won't call.

There's no sense in that, and anyway I have no reception. The stores of Kfar Saba are shuttered and boxes of bread and crates of milk are wrapped in plastic and waiting outside of restaurants and cafés.

Soon parents will start waking children for kindergarten and school, preparing the usual sandwiches, giving out the usual orders, spurring them on with the same unchanging script. In the morning my father liked having eggs sunny-side up on black bread. He liked making the meal himself, two eggs, prepared separately, one after another. I liked having my eggs the way my father made them, and it took me some time to perfect his technique so that the yolks kept their shape without leaking and stayed just a little raw, to retain its flavor. Butter is an option but I've always preferred olive oil, just a drop. If you practice a lot, the egg can be dropped into the pan with one hand, but I never managed that. I would season only with salt, no black pepper. Some people like it, but I, like my father, preferred not to obscure the taste of the egg. When the white of the egg would start to harden he'd tilt the pan gently and with the spatula would spray the yolk with some of the sizzling oil, in order to sear the membrane.

I wasn't hungry, even though I hadn't eaten for a long while. I knew I'd have to have something soon; otherwise I'd pass out. Traffic picked up a bit as I approached Ra'anana Junction. They've built a mall there now and a few buildings with the sort of alphabet soup names that seem fitting for high-tech firms. Even the bus stops have been consolidated into a sort of central station. The stops, which were once benches beneath a strip of asbestos roof, had been converted into Plexiglas stops with new seating, but the stops were still arranged in the same order and the bus lines to Jerusalem remained as they were.

The bus was practically empty and on the radio they were running through the same recycled news and the weatherman said there was a chance of rain in the north and center of the country. I sat in the same seat and looked at the empty seat that Palestine had once occupied. I looked at her hair and waited for her to turn around, but she did not look in my direction. I wanted to get to my feet, holding on to the plastic handholds, and tell her simply that I was sorry. I'll wait for the passenger beside her to get off the bus and then she'll make some room for me, will scoot over to the window and watch the rain that isn't coming, and I'll hold her hand, soft and warm, and I'll hope that she isn't yearning for my death, that she isn't yearning for hers.

And now we have children of our own and I have to get presents for them before returning. Maybe I'll get them something from the toy store in the airport, and then even if I have no room left in my luggage I'll be able to take a bag on board, maybe even two, especially if I decide to check the rolling suitcase. I have a ton of time before the flight. I could head up to Jerusalem and come back down. I have the time. My mother is certainly on the way to the hospital and my brothers must already know. I have to buy presents that will make the kids happy, maybe earphones for my daughter, the big, noise-canceling ones, so that she can block out the rest of the world. And for the boys? What could make them the happiest and still be within my price range? It's Palestine's money, and with the penalty I was forced to pay in order to reschedule my flights, I've already exceeded the limit she set for me. But I have to get them good presents, maybe a

remote-control robot for the little guy? And maybe a helicopter for the bigger one? A present that he'll remember,
and in that way my return to the house will be preserved in
his memory forever. It's probably expensive, but I have to,
and I'll stretch the credit card to the max, and if Palestine
asks — and surely she won't ask — I'll tell her that my father
died and I just had to.

What will I buy my wife with her money? Maybe a
neck scarf? I looked at the spot where she had once sat
on the bus, and I saw the way she lifted her hair with one
delicate movement of her hand and watched her loop the
scarf around her neck and then let her hair fall back across
her shoulders. She's warmer now and she practically turns
around to whisper her thanks.

It'll be fine, I wanted to tell her, but what will be fine?
And how will it be fine? And how can the man who de-
stroyed her home take up the mantel of savior and guaran-
tor of her salvation? Now, too, I remained seated. It was
cold back then, and Palestine was without a coat. I'd hoped
that she'd be cozy on the bus and was worried that she'd be
chilled when we reached the frigid city of Jerusalem. When
we get to the central bus station I'll offer her my jacket, I
thought, and maybe that will grant us a moment of intimacy.

Palestine never wears short sleeves. She has a scar along
the outside of her left forearm. Once she said tersely that is
was the result of a fall from her bike, back when she was in
kindergarten. I wanted to think otherwise. Maybe it was the
handiwork of her father, her brother, her cousin. I wanted
to think that I was her savior. In violation of my father's

orders I returned to Tira, determined to tell the truth and face the results. Palestine is not guilty. That's all I wanted to say, that I'd never met her, never heard of her, never been on the roof of the elementary school, middle school, or high school, as I'd written in the story. After the phone call from my father, news from Tira started streaming in, news that I ardently sought out, news that informed me that Palestine was real. There was a girl by that name, from a different neighborhood, who'd gone to a different school and who was known by her nationalistic birth name to only a select few people. The story I'd written a year earlier somehow was brought to the gates of the village. My older brother said he'd heard that one of the printing press workers was from Tira and had seen a copy of the journal during printing, while a different family member said that a Jewish journalist had hired a local Arab handyman and had asked him about me and showed him the journal. The handyman recognized the family name and the high school and was shocked that someone would dare to act that way in a school. Or maybe it was just a local man of letters who likes to stay up-to-date on current Hebrew poetry and prose and therefore subscribes to the journal. One way or another, once it was discovered, my story about Palestine was printed hundreds of times and sent to nearly every fax machine in Tira and placed at the doors of the mosques in advance of Friday prayers. Above the actual story, which was printed in full and in Hebrew and credited me as the author, the person who distributed it added, in Arabic: "An Unabashed Act of Harlotry in Tira: How Low Can We Go?" Because otherwise no one would have taken the time to read it.

I learned, from the details I was able to squeeze out of my brother, that the story had become the hot topic in Tira and that my father was fielding dozens of calls a day from people seeking to confirm that what they had heard was true. As far as the residents were concerned, the story was no work of fiction; it was an exposé of a shameful act conducted with the daughter of a respectable, God-fearing family from Tira. Palestine was the main point of interest, not me but rather this rumor of a licentious young woman who thought she could carry out dishonorable deeds without punishment. People in Tira loved hearing of loose girls; it strengthened their faith in the justness of their own ways. The men loved hearing about women who were caught, hoping that the subsequent onslaught and the indelible stain would serve as a warning to their wives and daughters. And the women—who according to my mother did nothing at the mourners' tents and bridal henna ceremonies besides talk about the publication of the horror story about Palestine and her family—were happy to slaughter a sacrificial lamb so long as it promised to keep the slander at bay and reinforced their sense of their own virtue.

The imams told the story from the pulpits, illustrating the way that immorality gnaws away at the foundations of society, yet another sign of the weakening of faith, a distancing from the morals of the Quran, a trend that must be halted at once. It was, they said, a "plague" that must be treated before it took hold of all of our daughters, tarnishing their honor, their purity, their chastity. My father, so I understood from my brother and mother, was running around from sheikh to imam, telling them that it hadn't happened, that it was only a story, and that Palestine was a made-up character that his son had never met and that he never imagined there was actually a girl who answered to that very same name. Palestine, for crying out loud, and is he so dumb, my son, as to reveal this sort of relationship with a woman on the pages of a newspaper? Were it the truth, he easily could have made up any other name; yet he chose Palestine, the homeland, not the woman. Dad conceded that the story was wretched and slanderous and detrimental to the cause of the homeland, and he told members of the local council that he had no idea what I was thinking when I wrote it, especially since he knows me to be a person whose political orientation is focused on the welfare of his own people. This awful story has nothing to do with any young woman from Tira, and he had no desire to tarnish the honor of a respectable local girl who had not sinned.

He also tried to speak with Palestine's parents, sent friends as mediators, but they returned empty-handed, stating that the parents of the girl had no interest in meeting my father.

And my father said that there's nothing that can be done, that it has nothing to do with me or the story that I wrote or the truth at large. When people want to believe something, nothing will change their minds, and the people have already decided that Palestine is a whore. And my brother, who was back in the village on college break, said that Palestine was his age and that he hadn't known that that was her name and that she was a beautiful girl, the prettiest in her class, with a long neck and eyelashes like no one else, just as in the story, and he told me that she had gotten engaged to her beloved before graduating from high school and that all of the girls in class were jealous of her because her fiancé, one of the first accountants in the village, built her the fanciest house in Tira. Not like the ones I remembered from my childhood, not a house on stilts and not a house with a red-tile roof but one of those modern villas that the newly rich villagers had started to build, once they'd hired architects and designers and poured time and money into houses, which would, they hoped, accentuate their wealth. When the story hit Tira, Palestine had been married for over six months, and her husband, who was twenty-eight and the son of a landowning family that sold stores for rent, arranged the most lavish wedding Tira had ever known. Once the story started to make the rounds in the village, Palestine went back to her parents' house, and one month later she was divorced.

When I returned to Tira, rather than going to my parents' house I went straight to the home of the sheikh who headed the sulha reconciliation committee in the village. I presented myself before the committee head and he mumbled a few words of prayer and requests for forgiveness, and when I swore to him that I had never seen Palestine, that I knew not of her existence and that I had never spoken a word to her, he said that he believed me but that it was too late and there was nothing to do but ask for forgiveness and mend my ways. But this is unjust, I said. She has done nothing wrong and does not deserve any sort of punishment. If anyone should be punished, it's me. The sheikh intoned that he saw no way to right the wrong other than for me to take Palestine's hand in marriage. But we didn't do anything, I said yet again. And again he repeated that he believed me, but I knew that he did not. We didn't sin, but if a wedding is what will right this wrong, I am willing to marry her. May God bless you, he said. Only in that way will you blot out the sin, and if you mend your ways then you will yet earn God's forgiveness.

I didn't know if I felt guilty or just wanted to be the good boy again, the studious one who never spoke about sex or girls with his classmates, who religiously took the right way to and from school. I didn't know if I'd offered to marry Palestine because I had begun to fall in love with her, just as I had when I conjured her on paper. Maybe I wanted her to think that I was a noble person, willing to correct a dreadful mistake and save her from Tira, from a husband who did not believe her and a backward family that did not have the decency to stand by her side. And maybe her husband loved her dearly and did not believe a word that the neighbors said but was left no choice? Maybe doubt had eaten into his heart and he realized that he could not trust a single person in this world? Sometimes I think that what he wanted was for her to stay but that she was ashamed, humiliated by the damage done to his honor, which was, through no fault of his own, flattened by rampant stories that she realized would forever taint her, her beloved, and their children. And she went to him, kissed him, told him that she loved him, that she would never love another person but him, and then returned to her parents' home and asked for a divorce.

That very day the sheikh showed up at my parents' house and said that an agreement had been reached. Later, I headed out with my new wife to Jerusalem, and my father, who drove up to the bus stop in Kfar Saba, handed me a fifty-shekel note and whispered that he never wanted to see me again. And in fact there was rain slanting down that morning and the weatherman on the bus radio reported that there was a chance of snow in Jerusalem, but that the window of opportunity was small.

F

1

I don't want to finish the story about my father. When I'm done he won't be with me anymore as he has been during the past few months since my return from Kfar Saba. As long as I'm writing, he's here with me. As long as I'm writing, I'm still with him, watching him wake and fall back into sleep, serving him water when he asks. As long as I continue writing, I will continue to talk to him, to tell him stories, to ask to hear his. As long as I'm writing, thinking of the next sentence, tinkering and editing, he still exists.

When I was a kid I never understood why it was that the dead were buried, why they were not left in their homes. So what if they don't talk or breathe? The important thing is that their body remains, and I, the child, can slip into bed beside my father's body. Later I learned that bodies rot and disintegrate, that parents can't be left to lie in their bedrooms and that you can't hide in their arms every time you're scared of the dark. And I started to think about what's inside of graves and to understand that in the end all that's left are bones, and that worms eat the flesh faster than we think, and that after a short while all that remains are the hair and the nails, which can grow even after death and once the dead are put in their graves. I didn't understand why in Tira the bodies are not put in caskets as they are in American movies, so that the worms won't be able to get near the body and it will remain whole, but soon enough I learned that a casket is of no use, even if it's made of steel.

When we were taught in third-grade history about the pharaohs and the mummies, I was happy to hear about embalming, and I wondered why it was that our parents are not mummified. And when we were in fourth grade, Kauthar, who was an average student, lost her father to a mysterious disease and I was petrified that this disease would strike other fathers and eventually reach mine. I wanted to tell Kauthar about mummification, but it was already too late. She didn't come to school for seven days and when she returned her father was already interred in the earth, because Muslims bury on the day of death, and surely his nails were already long.

As long as I write, I mummify my father, and his body, albeit old and sick, remains whole and beside my desk. My father's life is in my hands; I can keep him alive. When I decide that I'm done, when I Accept All Changes and save a final copy, I'll be sending my father to the cemetery in Tira, to the worms.

At night I return to the funeral that I didn't attend. To the ritual bathing ceremony that the men in the family likely held in the living room. That same raised wooden gurney that I once saw being brought into the home of my uncle, who died when I was in fifth grade. Muslims bury their dead on their sides, not their backs. They must certainly have mumbled prayers and repeated "Allah Akbar" as they

brought the wooden coffin—the only one in Tira—into my
parents' home. And where was Mom? The body is naked
when washed and the stomach is pressed on a few times
to release gas or any last secretions, and then they clean
the ears and the nose and seal the orifices with cotton. A
single, thorough wash and then they top it off with a total
of seven washes because seven is holy, and in this way are
you purified for the angels, whom you meet as soon as you
are laid in your grave. And then you must answer the questions of the angels, questions that determine your fate after
death: whether you are hell- or heaven-bound. And when
I was young, I was so scared that I would not be able to
answer correctly. "Who is your God?" the angels of the
grave ask. And you must answer: "God is my God." "And
who is your prophet?" And you must answer "Muhammad
is my prophet." But it isn't all that simple they told us in
religion class; don't think it's as simple as that. Only the true
believer is able to answer correctly. The infidel is incapable
of answering, and he whose heart is riddled with doubt will
stutter and fall mute from fear when he senses the arrival of
the angels. The angels bestow tranquility on the believers,
delivering white light and a divine solace, a guarantee that
you have arrived at the promised land, while the hearts of
the impure and the hearts of the nonbelievers are filled with
dread, a terror that we cannot even begin to comprehend.
When such a person is stricken in this way, tongue-tied and
incapable of answering their questions, he is pounded by
angels and driven with blows to the depths.

   They surely pushed the couches to the corner of the
living room, covered the television screen with a white sheet,
moved the colorful vases with the plastic plants, and then

placed my father on the washing board. The bevy of swans
floating across a pond in a foreign land looked on at the
ceremony from their spot within a frame on the wall, wit-
nessing my father's final moments in his home. Are they
still there, the swans? I wanted to ask my mother or one of
my brothers. And had the couches been replaced already
several times over, the living room painted a different color?

After the cleansing ceremony the deceased is wrapped
in white shrouds with only his face bare, and my father
smiled. They didn't touch his lips. It was in a smile I could
have sworn. It had to have been a smile and not an expression of fear. My father is not afraid of death, no matter what
he might have said. He died placidly. He had to have died
placidly, at one with his fate.

And people surely congregated in the courtyard —
relatives, friends, and neighbors — and waited for the first-
degree relatives to plant kisses on the forehead and the
cheeks, caresses and final glances. My mother certainly
sobbed — and my nephews? I hope they kept them away,
didn't let them see the body. They're still young. I remember that I didn't sleep for nights on end after I saw a casket
being brought out of the neighbor's house. And maybe they
no longer tell tales of demons to the kids, and the dead no
longer scare the young?

How many people attended my father's funeral? Multitudes?
Was it impressive? Or was it attended only by a smattering
of people, relatives and friends who were compelled to be
present lest they be spoken ill of. For this wasn't the death
of a young man, or the result of a terrible disaster, or the

passing of a very senior official. Maybe no one showed up and only my three brothers served as pallbearers, leaving one corner of the casket unsupported, wobbling, with Dad inside, all the way to the graveyard? Perhaps no one showed up on my account and no one said a final prayer for him, and once his casket was brought into the mosque the usual worshippers left and my brothers, who do not know how to pray, were left with no imam and no sheikh to guide them. Muslims bury quickly, as though eager to get rid of the body. They do not wait for distant relatives to arrive and do not don special clothes; mourners may come straight from construction sites and from the fields, their shoes muddy, their clothes dirty, their hands stained. And at the end of the burial ceremony the crowd disperses and the sons of the deceased sit for three days in a mourning tent and receive the consolers. The men and women are separated. My three brothers would have sat there, rising to their feet whenever a new consoler entered. It was the end of January, cold and rainy, so the space would be lined with electric coil heaters, which produced only meager heat because the electricity in Tira is always weak and incapable of powering the heaters at full blast. They did not shave for three days; they shook hands; they delivered set and predictable responses to the standard condolences. They served black coffee in disposable plastic cups and sent around baskets of dates to sweeten the bitter coffee and to ensure the health of those who remained alive.

Mom likely received the female well-wishers in the living room of the house, where my father's body had until recently lain. Mom definitely did not have patience for the ladies of the neighborhood and the relatives, who consoled her for a minute and then launched into a full hour of gossip. Who is marrying whom, who absconded with whose wife, who cheated on her husband, who fought with her mother-in-law. She only wanted to be beside my brothers and yet she would not see them until the late hours of the night when all of the strangers had left, and the men of the family were once again able to meet the women. And did my mother feel my absence then?

I was not there at the end of the evening, with my mother, in order to make the nephews laugh, the little ones who had just lost the grandfather in whose house they had grown up and from whom they had heard stories and with whom they had eaten oranges in the winter, which he knew how to peel so that the peel was one long spiral and could be played with like a Slinky. And I wasn't there to see the way in which the refuse was released from his intestines and the gas from his stomach, and I wasn't there to touch him, to caress his hand and kiss his forehead, for my heart to burn as his casket was taken from the living room, for my breath to catch as he was lowered to the earth, for the terror of death to tie my tongue when the sand covered him.

2

Ever since that story about Palestine, I'm incapable of making up stories. The childhood memories that I added to the life stories of my clients were taken from the bank of my own pleasant memories: when it seemed to me that one of my clients had had a sad childhood, I would add to his life the smell of holiday cakes that Mom used to make, and when I felt that one of the clients had lacked friends, then I offered up some of my sweeter memories from grade school. When a woman neglected to mention her Arab neighbors in Jerusalem before the war, I volunteered my own cheerful neighbors.

With every contribution from my memory something in me faded. I knew that the comfort that I derived from raising the memory up from the depths would never again be as it had been. These were feelings that I embedded in other people's stories, childhood memories that I had to re-create, edit, and tailor to the lives of my clients, fitting them into the right time frame, the right period, language, village, town, neighborhood, and home in which they lived. When I added the memory of a babka cake that the client's mother never made, I gave away my memory of the trays of rice and sweet milk my mother used to make on the eves of Ramadan, and from the moment I wrote that memory as part of the life of a Holocaust survivor, the longing no longer bubbled up within me. True, I saved the files on my computer and the hard copies in my office, and I could always return to my own memories in these books, but I had given them up, and they could never again arouse in me the same feelings they once had.

I donated each of my pleasant childhood and adolescent memories until they were all gone, and all that remained were the bad memories, which, ever since my marriage to Palestine, I'd begun to find solace in. There was no more space for the pleasant ones: I was not worthy of them. The residents of Tira were not worthy of them. The good memories no longer coincided with my life story.

The memory of foraging for za'atar in the hills I now planted in the life stories of new immigrants. And rather than keeping the scent of the silvery green herb, I retained only the fear of the nature inspectors. The memory of watching my father's perfect shave was given to a cancer patient, my youngest client, who died at age fifty after a long struggle with the disease, which first struck when he was in high school. The spiritually uplifting feeling of riding in my father's lap in the driver's seat as we cruised through the fields I gave to the life stories of the old warriors, who never mentioned, when speaking into the mic, their love of their small children.

And with every pleasant memory that I relinquished, Tira was emptied of its good people. The warmth was replaced with violence, the smiles with threatening grimaces. The love stories that I used to hear in my youth were erased, and in their place stood only memories of the murder of women. The neighbors' willingness to help was swapped for bitter feuds, the blessings and salutations for pistols and rifles, the family ties for inheritance wars, and the games of hide-and-seek for land quarrels. The pride that Dad tried to instill in us is something I can no longer feel. In its place, I sense only a sour breeze, the shameful feeling of having lost. The hope of eventual victory, come what may, has been swapped for the knowledge that defeat shall forever be my fate.

With every memory that I wove into a life story that was not mine, Tira, the home I loved, became the most terrifying place. The place that I longed to return to became a dark and threatening place in my mind, a place I didn't dare visit.

Brothers can kill one another, the neighbors do not speak with one another, love is forbidden, and hope has been drained from the hearts of the inhabitants. There are no more fig trees, no grapes, and no strawberries, only homes ringed with tall walls isolating the residents. The rich are in big houses, the poor in small ones, the entire place is overcrowded and stifling, and there is no longer room for games of hide-and-seek in the neighborhood and no one participates anymore or commits themselves to the continuation of the struggle on Land Day. There are no longer processions on Sabra and Shatila Day, and no one remembers, and what was that anyway? A few thousand dead, a drop in the sea when compared to the number of victims these days.

The spring does not come to the Tira of my memory; nothing blooms there and there are no bees to be caught in bags of juice. The only trees remaining in the village are fruitless trees, bare of foliage, growing only thorny branches to be used for whipping little children.

There is only one pleasant memory left from Tira, one I knew I would not donate to any of my clients, and it was

on account of that story that a small part of me still longed
to return, knowing deep down inside that things could yet
be righted, that Tira would always be the only place on
earth I'd truly love, a place where I could find security and
tranquility, as I can only imagine that security and tranquility might feel.

In the memory I kept for myself, I am standing on the roof
of the high school, on the eve of Independence Day, looking out on the fields that once were, and then, suddenly, up
onto the roof comes a girl so beautiful that it is enough to
look at her once and know that life has a purpose. A soft
breeze teases her long black hair, and her large eyes seem
to have been created with natural kohl, long eyelashes and
delicate red lips. She is like Layla from "Layla and Majnun"
and like the women in the poetry of Imru' al-Qais, and yet
she is from Tira. And she is standing before me, looking at
me determinedly as she whispers so that only I will hear
her: "Come."

3

يابا

نعم يابا

وجيه بعده فاتح؟

مين وجيه، الحلاق؟

الحلاق.

الله يرحمه وجيه، صاره ميت اكثر من خمس سنين، ليه؟

لا ولا أشي، مرات بافطن له. الله يرحمه

شعرك طويل. بدو حلاقه. عند مين بتحلق بامريكا؟

كل مره غير. فش حلاق ثابت

بنفعش هيك. الحلاق اللحام، والميكانيكي لازم يكونوا ثابتين. لحيتي

طويله انا، ولا احسن هيك، بلكي تخربطوا الملائكه بالقبر وفكروني إخوان؟

تقلش هيك يابا من شان الله.

استوى العدس شكله يابوي.

بتعرف قديش صار لي مش سامع استوى العدس؟

ليه، بأميركا فش عدس؟

مبلا فيه, جربت مره اعمل للاولاد، بس الصغير اكل شوي

مجروش؟

أه، مجروش.

عصرت عليه حبة ليمون؟

أه، زبط معي بس الأولاد مش متعودين.

فجل؟ شوربة العدس بتتاكلش بدون فجل.

باعرف، والله بعرف، وتحسرت يومها نسبت اشتري فجل. على ايش

بتضحك؟

اخخخ، باضحك من شر البلية ,يابا. وهذه أكيد ما سمعتها من سنين، مش هيك؟

لا عندجد، شو اللي ضحكك؟

فطنت للعدس والفجل. بايامها بسجن الدمون فتحنا بأضراب عن الأكل. كنا بدنا يسمحوا لنا بترنزيستور، جرايد، كتب، زيارات وهيك امور. اضربنا والله اكثر من أسبوعين والإداره وافقوا على اغلب المطالب، بس مش الكل.

أبو الوليد، متذكره؟ من كفر كنا، قال بدنا عدس، بدون عدس مجروش وفجل ما في اتفاق.

وافقوا؟

وافقوا. والله ازكا عدس اكلته بحياتي. شو ضحكنا ضحك، واحنا مش قادرين نضحك، مش قادرين نقف على رجلينا. من يومها وانا احب العدس وصرت احب اطبخه.

أيام الشتويه.

العدس بس بالشتويه، لو أولادك عندي كنت بتشوف كيف بدهم ياكلوا من عداساتي.

مالك يابا.

ولا أشي يابا ولا اشي. احسن لهم هيك، احسن لهم هناك. شو بدهم بوجع هالقلب.

صعب هناك.

هون اصعب.

يابا.

بتنادي كثير يابا.

خلص تعبت؟

لا، احكي.

بايش بتفكر قبل ما تنام؟

مش فاهم.

في أشي ثابت بتفكر فيه، بتسرح فيه قبل ما تغفى؟

ما أنت عارف، بنام مع راديو شغال صار لي خمسين سنه عشان ما افكر باشي.

بس مرات الراديو ببث موسيقى، فش أخبار بالليل وأكيد في سرحات بتساعدك تنام.

بأيام السلم؟

ليه؟ في فرق بين السلم والحرب؟

بالسلم مرات بفكر، وبلهي حالي بحركات شطرنج ومرات بتخيل حالي لعيب فطبول.

بأيام الحرب؟

بأيام الحرب بتخيل حالي جندي، حامل بروده قديمه، وهاجم لحالي هيك على دبابات.

وبتنتصر؟

وانا راسي على المخده؟

اه.

طبعا. كل ليله.

I have to find a way to translate the last conversation with Dad. Have to find a way to translate the saying "the lentils are fully cooked." Have to find a way of translating the pain when I tried to slide the thongs on his swollen feet. I have to find a way of translating his final smile.

I have to transcribe it all, before I start to write. Word for word. If there's a word I can't make out I'll go back and listen again. I'll press Stop, I'll rewind the tape, and I'll do it again.

4

"They're coming, they're coming, Mom. Mom, they're going to get us," I type out the last sentences my father spoke.

Everything's okay, Dad. Everything's okay, I'm here.

We have to escape fast. They're coming, they're coming from the direction of the orchards, Mom. They're cutting off people's heads. Mom, we have to go.

Dad, everything's okay. Dad, do you want a sip of water?

We have to run, I remember, they're beheading little children, too.

What's wrong, my beloved son, assam Allah alik.

I saw my father, Mom. I saw him. I saw him fall. I saw the whole thing. The blood, the brains, and I saw you screaming, and I saw the neighbors come. We have to go, Mom.

Dad, please, Dad, everything's okay. We're here in the hospital. You're just dreaming. Here, Dad, have a sip of water.

I slipped the straw into my father's mouth, his sunken eyes closed, and when he was done taking tiny measured sips he gently patted the back of my hand, which held the straw steady between his cracked lips.

The spools on my recorder continued to turn in silence. The brown tape, most of which was filled with silences and my attempts at prompting, was finished. I let the silence play until the button popped up to announce the end of side A.

My father lay there unanimated. I called him quietly so as not to wake up any of his roommates, and he did not answer. His body was hot. I brought my right cheek to his mouth and held my breath so I could feel his on my flesh.

And like a professional documentarian, I flipped the cassette to the B-side and continued to record the silence in my father's room and the arrival of the nurse. I held my father's hand, and the nurse, who pressed a stethoscope to his chest for several seconds, pressed a button and then more nurses and doctors arrived, and my father lay there so beautifully, in silence, his eyes shut, and I waited for him to open them and to address me.

~~Are you his son?~~
   ~~Yes~~
   ~~Should we resuscitate?~~
   ~~Yes, of course.~~
   ~~One, two . . . I feel the bones crumbling.~~
   ~~That's it, no more.~~
   ~~Are you sure?~~
   ~~Yes, please, it's enough.~~
   ~~Time of death: two thirty-seven.~~
My father died peacefully, in his sleep, the sort of death that comes like a kiss. I held his still-warm and pleasant hand. "Dad," I called to him. "Dad." And he only tightened his hand around mine for a second. I could have sworn that his smile, which had never been so tranquil, spread as soon as he relinquished his grip.

Dad, I am so sorry. I know that I stole your memory, and I am so sorry. I didn't know then the power of a happy memory. I didn't know what happens when a pleasant memory is written down, stolen, borrowed, or loaned to others.

Yes, I admit, I remembered the story of that Independence Day from your youth.

I remember well how we'd set out for the field to pick figs, once the afternoon had taken the edge off the summer sun. I remember that you used to say that figs should be picked in the morning and afternoon, because they ripen fast, and should be picked twice a day from the tree otherwise the overly ripe ones will fall to the ground and rot. And I remember that you said I mustn't be afraid of snakes and how you were always happy to find a freshly shed snakeskin, and you'd say, "It hasn't even had a chance to dry out yet." And you'd lift it up on the tip of a stick, as though you were still a child. And only out in the field did I see how you were as a kid, fearless, the child from Grandma's stories who was never scared and who used to sneak out of the village on a bike even when it was under curfew and who would cling to the ladder on the back of the bus that came through the village in the mornings and evenings, taking the workers to and from work, the scrappy kid with the relatively small frame who did not hesitate to get mixed up in the kids' wars. And I was scared even when you told me that I had no reason to fear snakes when I was wearing my boots, because snakes are generally not poisonous and are more likely to be scared of humans and slink away.

And I remember, Dad, what you told me that summer. I remember you up in the fig tree, one of the two trees at the edge of the vineyard, and though I'd seen you climb that tree hundreds of times I was always afraid that you'd stumble and fall. We were by ourselves in the fields, far from the houses of the village, which inched closer and swallowed up the grasses with every passing summer until they ringed the fig trees. And you asked me not to tell a soul. "Do you promise?" you asked. And I swore by God not to tell, and I know that you told me because you wanted me to stop being afraid. You wanted me to have friends. And you asked if there was a girl in the class who I looked at differently from all the others, and you were disappointed when I said no, even though I was lying, because there was one girl that I looked at differently. But I was afraid to admit it because I was afraid of the religion teacher and of God and I feared that if I admitted it I'd turn into one of those bad children with a foul mouth and unfinished homework. And I remembered you standing on a branch and hanging up the blue bucket with the yellow handle, the one that sometimes held cleaning fluid and was then thoroughly washed and served as a basket for transporting fresh figs. It was there that you told me of your first kiss, how on an Independence Day vacation you went up to the roof of the school to uproot the flag of Israel that had been planted there in a barrel full of sand.

I remember you told me how surprised you were to find the prettiest girl in the school, the prettiest girl in the village, the prettiest girl in the world, on the roof of the school, the girl you looked at differently from all of the other girls, and that she smiled at you bashfully and that you were the happiest person in the world. I remember that you were picking figs as you told me the story and how in that moment you were once again a young man on the roof of the school on Independence Day, discovering how love can feel and how you said that you understood then, without knowing how to put it into words, the reason why people are born. The beautiful girl carried in her hand a flag that she had drawn herself, and she was the last person you'd expect to find climbing up on the roof on her own: barefoot, the bashful girl, with the long neck and the loose hair, who now sought to plant the flag in the place of the one you had uprooted and you said that you blocked her path, smiling, and that she asked you to move and you refused.

"It's against the law," you told her. And she laughed softly and said, "I'm a criminal, just like you, so get out of my way."

"I'll tell on you," he must have threatened her, when she tried to bypass him. Did she allow you to hold her hand as she tried to plant the flag of Palestine in the barrel? Both of you looked around, verifying that you were alone, under the skies of Independence Day eve, and the great humiliation that would soon come in the form of fireworks lighting the nearby skies of Kfar Saba. And maybe you asked and maybe you did not, but she brought her lips close to yours, and you felt that your heart was about to fall out, and she drove the flag into the sand of the barrel. Rushing, you felt something strange, different, perhaps elation? And a great sorrow suddenly flooded your heart when she said that she was ashamed that she was happier than ever before, on this night, the night that marks the destruction.

I didn't like eating figs, and I was always afraid when you peeled them and ate them and said they were the best thing in the world, because there were many different varieties of figs, the names of which you knew. I was afraid of figs, especially dreams of figs, because I remember well that Grandma and our aunts, who were then still on good terms and were not yet fighting over land and inheritances, I remember them saying that the eating of figs in a dream is a bad sign, a sign of certain death.

1

Americans don't pronounce the *l* in the salmon that Palestine ordered for dinner. I wasn't hungry, but I had to order
something, so I chose the mushroom risotto from the list of
appetizers. Our daughter promised not to hole up in her
room as she usually does and said she'd watch her brothers
until they go to bed and then make sure that they were sleeping peacefully. "Please," I begged of her in ~~Hebrew~~ Arabic.
"Leave the door open and try not to wear earphones, in case
your little brother wakes up." She merely nodded, and I
was unable to see if she was happy or sad or angry that her
mother and I were going out alone to eat for the first time.

I so wanted beer, from the tap, and maybe a little whiskey or
a vodka chaser, with a preference for vodka, but I ordered a
glass of white wine once Palestine said that, yes, please, she
would like some wine with her fish. A bottle? I suggested.
And she said no, a glass would be fine because she had to
work the next morning but that I could order a bottle if I
preferred. I made do with a glass of house wine, a chardon-
nay. I so wanted to drink, quickly and in a single gulp, three
shots of whiskey or vodka, neat. I didn't know if we'd raise
our glasses and drink to life. Palestine would never initiate
that sort of gesture, and I was embarrassed to do that now,

after so many years of marriage. "Bsakhtek," I whispered
to myself in Arabic as I raised the glass to my lips for a first
sip, and then I said, "Nice restaurant." And I looked around
the place, which had gotten the highest rating on a tourism
site that rates restaurants by user-generated reviews.

"Yes, one of the best," Palestine said and added that it
was a restaurant that visiting professors and lecturers are
taken to when they come to visit the university, revealing
that it was not her first visit and that the risotto I ordered was
not bad at all and that she had even considered ordering it,
but that since she'd already had it several times she thought
she might try something else, even though she usually sticks
to what she knows and likes.

I tried to temper the heat that flared in my mind once I
realized that as opposed to what I had thought, this was not
the first time that my daughter had been asked to watch the
boys while Palestine had gone out to dinner. The notion that
she had a life that I knew nothing about fogged my thoughts
to the point that I considered aborting the conversation I had
planned and that I still had no clear idea of how to initiate
or what I might say during it.

Maybe it's better that way: We'll just talk about the
kids, maybe about the restaurant, Palestine's plans for the
future. Maybe I'll even let her pay as she likes to do when
we go out with the kids to McDonald's. After all, it's her
money, and it would be ridiculous for me to pay as I had
planned, like a high schooler who's been saving up to take
his girlfriend out to the movies and a proper restaurant for
the first time.

"How's the book coming along?" she asked me, catching me unprepared, and I couldn't remember if I'd told her

that I was working on my father's book. No, certainly not, it made no sense that I would have said anything. I'd told no one about the recording and the transcription.

"Slowly," I said, hoping that she was referring to the book I always talk about when I'm asked what I'm up to in town and I say, "Working on a book." Could it have been a barbed comment, though her face showed no sign of malice?

Maybe she asked about the book just so that I would soothe her and say that I wasn't writing a thing. It's quite possible that she intuited that my writing would always be disastrous for her.

We never spoke about the story or my desire to write, aside from my writing gigs at the paper and for clients. Did she even read the story back then? All of a sudden, I was filled with curiosity and wanted to ask her if she'd read it. Or had someone just told her the gist of it, a plot summary, not that there was a plot but rather what was considered in Tira to have been the heart of the story, in other words, the fact that I'd slept with her. Was she even asked to issue a denial? Who asked her? Perhaps her parents? Who first told her of the story? Her husband? And maybe she was handed a copy, asked to read, as they stood around her and waited for her response. Did they believe her? Did she believe herself? Did she even know who I was?

It's a small village, after all, and people know one another even when they aren't really acquainted. Did she know my name and think that an affirmative answer would be seen as an admission? Or did she say no, she had no idea who I was, that this was the first time she'd heard the name and expressed wonder at why someone was serving this text to her to read and say that she has no idea why this thing, written in Hebrew, has anything to do with her life. Maybe it took her a few moments before she realized that the charges were severe. Maybe it took some time until she realized that she was being put on trial, that they were waiting for the sound of her voice, an utterance, and that no matter what it produced, her verdict was sealed.

And maybe she actually liked the story? I banished the notion immediately, even though it made me happy. Maybe she read it and loved it, just as I fell in love as I wrote? Just as I fall in love every time I read the copy that I clipped out of the journal in which it was published, a copy that I kept, laminated, hidden, and taken with me wherever I go? A copy that I folded up back in Jerusalem and tucked into my ID case that I took everywhere and that when we moved here I tucked into the pages of my passport. Once every few weeks I take the story out of its hiding spot, feel it between my fingers, check in on the faded page, make sure that the words are still legible among the folds. At times I've considered photocopying the page or taking a picture of it with my cell phone, in case the copy is lost, but I've never done that, and I've never possessed more than the original copy, taken from the two complimentary issues I was given upon publication.

I so wanted to throw away that copy of the story, which I could recite by heart, but I was not able to. The fierce desire to forget, as though it never were, clashed with the fear that its words would fall out of order and be forgotten until my only recollection of them would be hazy.

And since I did not know if Palestine had read it or what she thought of what she had read, I saved the copy in case she would one day ask to read the story. Or perhaps she would prefer that I read it to her, and maybe she would like it and would think of me as a writer and would urge me to continue writing in order to find out what befalls the two lovers.

I look at Palestine, who is called that way only by me, albeit mostly in my mind because I rarely say her name aloud, and wonder, what does she recall of the day of our wedding, if one can call the forced signing of paperwork before the sheikh by that name? Does she remember the rain? And that she was cold? Does she remember where she sat on the bus and what she thought about during the ride? And the snow, does she remember the snow that fell on Jerusalem the following day?

I ditch the name and start in midsentence. "Is it good?" I ask and watch her eat her salmon dish, and she answers with a slight nod. She's so different, I think to myself and immediately banish the thought. I can't. I can't go into this now; it's all that's left. She's beautiful, so beautiful. She eats and I remember her back and her hair flowing over her shoulders, and so quickly I am able to see Palestine from the story, the lass folded into the pages of my passport, the folds only making her more attractive. She is before me in all her splendor on the roof of the high school in Tira, on the top of the school that is no longer a high school, because instead of one junior high in the village there are today four of them and three high schools, which I read about on the local news sites, looking for the kids from my class, for their offspring, who surely resemble them and must have taken their spots in the assorted classes. Do the good students still sit up front and are the lazy ones still relegated to the back?

"What's the story?" It was Palestine asking.

"What?"

"You're not eating?"

"You think the kids are okay?" I asked, and she responded that if anything was wrong they would have called. And I wanted to tell her that I didn't mean now, at this moment, but that I wanted to know if they are alright, that I wanted for her to tell me that they're fine and will be fine. I wanted to ask her if she knows whether or not the kids have childhood memories, even though they're still children, and I wondered whether kids know, in the midst of a certain event, that this will be part of the landscape of their memory. Is there a sign that informs the child that a certain event will be anchored in his mind and will be brought to the surface under certain circumstances or in an hour of exertion, when he starts to fear the terror of forgetfulness?

"What do they know, the kids?" I wanted to ask her. What do they think about me and her? And what do they know of themselves? What happens to kids who do not know their roots?

Palestine made quick work of her salmon. She said she'd been asked to extend her stay, offered the tenure-track position that she had so ardently sought.

"Why aren't you eating?" she asked me again, and I realized she had no intention of telling me anything beyond the fact that she's staying here and that I am free to do as I please.

"Palestine," I wanted to call her, to say her name aloud, what is your first memory?

Maybe she'd tell of a rainy day, of puddles on the way to school, of a new umbrella, like in the children's stories, and of an electric coil heater back in the day when electricity worked in the village even when it was raining and the way that her siblings would cluster around the heater, playing that game where you flip a ring on the back of your hand and jiggle it carefully so it doesn't fall and you win when you get it over the tip of your thumb. I wanted to ask her if she, too, fights a shapeless enemy at night, trying to defend her childhood home, or does she, perhaps, before sleep, travel back to her husband's house, replaying the moments of their falling in love, returning to the first touch and the first kiss, to her engagement, to her selection of a wedding dress, her makeup, her hair, her wedding day, the dances, at first men and women separately, until the moment when she was led onto the floor to dance with the groom, who was actually capable of dancing, stomping his feet and hopping with the rest of the men and delicate during their joint dance? Does she, before sleep, return to the moments of destruction? Do I appear to her as a monster, a power outage that darkens the house on a rainy day in Tira, causing the ring to fall from the back of her hand?

I could also have started the conversation with lines that I'd heard Arabs say in movies, "Let's turn over a new leaf." Or: "Let us not ask one another of the past." May I, after seventeen years, ask to erase our past? Or maybe the right opening line ought to be: "Let's edit our past from the beginning?" I'll tell you how I'd like you to remember me: a young writer whose passion for writing brought about a disaster that he never sought to bring upon you. Here we are, two victims, sitting at an American restaurant, where we know no one and no one knows us, and we're trying to start anew. You tell of how compassion replaced the terrible anger and the fathomless hatred that you once felt for me, how, with the years, the monster that you imagined me to be changed, how the lad from the school roof transformed from a rapist to someone in search of a love he had not yet known.

A young man whose father whispered into his ear on his wedding day that he would never know love and asked not to see him until the day he dies. What did your parents ask of you? What did they wish for you, either overtly or covertly? Would you go home if they summoned you? Have they asked and have you refused? Will you join your mother's funeral procession, observe the days of mourning for your father?

I wanted to tell her that ever since I met her I wanted to return her to her house; that during our first days together in Jerusalem I would imagine the two of us on the back of a white horse, a great strong, white horse whose hoofbeats would reverberate throughout Tira, striding slowly, confidently, fearing nothing, and she seated sidesaddle before me in a long white dress. The locals peering at us through cracked doors and shutters, our faces sealed and expressionless, just the footfalls of the horse telling of our victory. That we've won the war. My arms encircle her hips and gently hold the reins in my cut and bloody palms. And I look at her profile, her long hair, flowing over her shoulders and concealing her face, and occasionally a gentle wind tosses it and reveals some of the length of her neck, and I recall one of the few phrases I learned in classical Arabic, which describes the length of a woman's neck according to the earrings with which she can decorate her ears, and here she is, the woman from the Arabic class, seated before me on the horse, and the horse knows where to go, striding toward the house of her beloved, whom I had never seen, and stopping in front of an impressive villa behind a tall gate. And when the horse stops, she dismounts with a light movement and starts to walk back home, knowing that all will be as it once was, that no one will dare say a word, about her or about me, and she does not look back when she returns home. I wait for her to turn back toward me and for her gaze to express gratitude, but she goes inside and locks the door behind her and leaves me there, alone, on the back of the horse, which stands still before the house, not knowing which way to turn.

"It's starting to rain," Palestine said and looked out the window, as the rest of the diners also turned their eyes to the glass.

"At long last," I was glad to hear her say. She smiled. "Aren't you going to eat?"

POSTSCRIPT/ARABIC CHAPTER

Dad.

Yes, my son.

Is Wajiya still working?

Which Wajiya, the barber?

The barber.

Allah Yerhamo. Wajiya died more than five years ago. Why?

No, nothing. Sometimes I remember him, may his memory be a blessing.

Your hair is long. You need a haircut. Who cuts your hair for you in America?

A different person every time. There's no regular guy.

That's not the way things work. The barber, the butcher, the mechanic: they all have to be regulars. My beard is too long. I have to shave. Or maybe it's better this way so that the angels in the grave get confused and think I'm with the Muslim Brotherhood.

Don't talk that way, Dad, please.

It looks like the lentils are fully cooked, my son.

Do you know how long it's been since I've heard that expression, Dad?

Why, they don't have lentils in America?

Yes, they do. I tried to make some for the kids. Only the little guy ate them.

Mashed?

Yes, mashed.

Did you squeeze lemon juice on it?

Yes, it came out good. It's just that the kids aren't used to it.

Did you have radish? You can't eat lentil soup without radish.

I know, believe me, I know. I was so distraught that I forgot to buy radish. What are you laughing at?

I'm laughing. Laughing out of distress. You probably haven't heard that one in a while, either, huh?

No, really, Dad. What's funny?

I remembered the lentils and the radishes. Back in the day in Damon Prison we went on a hunger strike. We wanted to be allowed transistors, newspapers, books, visits, that sort of thing. And we really did strike for more than two weeks and the authorities gave in to most of our demands but not all. Do you remember Abu al-Walid? From Kafr Kana. He said we demand lentils, and without mashed lentils and radishes there isn't going to be an agreement.

And did they agree?

They agreed. I swear I never ate a more delicious bowl of lentils. Wow, did we laugh, though we didn't even have the strength to laugh. Ever since then I love lentils and love cooking them.

In the winter.

Lentils are winter food. If your kids were with me, you'd see how they eat up my lentils.

What happened, Dad?

Nothing, my son. Nothing happened. They're better off there. What do they need this heartache for?

It's tough over there.

Here it's tougher.

Dad.

You say "dad" a lot.

Are you tired?

No. Go on.

Is there something you always think about before you fall asleep?

You know I sleep with the radio on. Fifty years I've been going to sleep with the radio on so that I don't have to think about a thing.

But sometimes the radio has music on. There are no news shows on at night and there must be something that you summon to help you drift off.

In times of peace?

Why is there a difference between times of peace and times of war?

In times of peace I sometimes replay chess moves, sometimes imagine myself in the middle of a soccer match.

And in times of war?

In times of war I see myself as a soldier, carrying an old rifle and charging alone toward the tanks.

And do you win?

When my head is on the pillow?

Yes.

Of course. Every night.